Will's right hand closed around the soft flesh of the Comanche's throat in a stroke of sheer blind luck, and suddenly he found himself staring into a pair of eyes slitted with hatred.

A chilling scream burst from the throat of Iron Horse as the two foes struggled for any advantage. Their faces were only inches apart, sinewy arms battling each other's strength, legs and feet thrashing for leverage on sun-baked soil. Will felt that renegade's incredible power drive him back to the ground. Locked in a deadly embrace with the Comanche, Will now understood the nature of his enemy. Iron Horse was part man, part animal. His animal instincts governed how the fight would be waged. He would kill his adversary any way he could. There would be no rules. . . .

RENEGADE

Frederic Bean

FAWCETT GOLD MEDAL · NEW YORK

A Fawcett Gold Medal Book
Published by Ballantine Books
Copyright © 1993 by Frederic Bean

Library of Congress Catalog Card Number: 92-97269

ISBN 0-449-14845-9

Manufactured in the United States of America

First Edition: May 1993

Chapter One

Santa Elena Canyon was quiet, empty. The Rio Grande flowed sluggishly along the canyon floor in late summer, walled on both banks by towering cliffs of stone. Offshoot canyons fed the river during the brief rainy seasons, but now they were dry, barren of all but the hardiest vegetation. Cactus and agave clung to thin topsoil. Slender mesquite trees bent sharply in the swirling canyon winds, thorny branches swaying in the irregular gusts. These far reaches of West Texas seldom saw any human activity, for the land was harsh, desertlike, untamed. Summer temperatures blazed above one hundred degrees from May until early October, a killing heat for men and horses where water was so scarce.

The silence ended when ten barefoot Comanche ponies entered the mouth of Santa Elena. The wiry little mustangs came single file down a narrow game trail, bearing copper-skinned men and deerhide slings carrying scant provisions. These warriors were not of the same blood, for they were outcasts from the five Comanche bands that once ruled the southwestern plains. Two were Penatekas. Three had been banished from the easternmost tribe, the Noconas. A lone Yamparika rode at the rear, watching their back trail. Just one fierce Kotsoteka was a member of the group, though his blood lust paled beside the remaining three who rode at the front of the quiet procession. These three had once been members of the Kwahadie band, the most warlike group of plains Indians on earth. For a hundred years of brutal warfare before the first white men came, the Kwahadies had driven off the savage Apache tribes to the west, and beaten the lowly

1

Lipans, and Kiowas, into peaceful submission to the north and east. Known for their extreme cruelty, other plains tribes gave them a wide berth.

At the front of this renegade group, an uncommonly tall warrior sat atop the withers of a sleek pinto mustang stallion. His deeply etched broad face swung back and forth as the pony carried him up the canyon, his hard black eyes taking in every detail of his surroundings. His Comanche name was Conas Woba-Poke, a string of words to describe the fire-horse-wagon ridden by the white man atop iron rails. A shortening of the name became Iron Horse.

Miles deep into Santa Elena Canyon, Iron Horse swung his pinto into an offshoot canyon angling northwest. Winding along the narrow passage, he watched the silent cliffs and listened to even the slightest sound. In one powerful hand he carried an ancient Spencer breech-loader carbine. A rusted Navy Colt .44 cap-and-ball revolver was tucked in the horse-hair belt of his beaded deerskin leggings. Guns were the reason he rode up this canyon. Diente Oro had promised him a trade for many repeating rifles. Iron Horse did not completely trust Diente Oro, named for the gold tooth in the front of his mouth. Gold Tooth Valdez was as treacherous as the worst white men. But he was also a Comanchero, a man who traded weapons to the Comanches. And over the past few years, those weapons had become precious to Iron Horse and his dwindling band of followers. Bluecoat soldiers hounded them in increasing numbers, and they had repeating rifles. Iron Horse knew that he must have similar guns if he meant to lead successful raids against the white-skinned enemy.

The canyon walls closed around the renegades as they moved up the narrow niche. At a bend in the passage Iron Horse halted his pony and sat quietly, awaiting the signal to proceed. For a time the canyon was silent. A pony stamped its hoof impatiently. Another swished away flies with its tail.

A whistle, like that of a night hawk, came from somewhere high on the canyon rim. Iron Horse gave the sign of a closed fist, then he heeled his mustang forward, around the turn.

The Comanches entered a wide bowl in the canyon, eroded by many centuries of wind and water. Rock walls hundreds of feet high jutted above the basin floor. Scattered across the bottom of the wide spot in the canyon, half a dozen adobe huts reflected the sun's glare. A stand of cottonwood trees encircled a precious, life-giving spring in the middle of the basin. Iron Horse paid little attention to the huts, or the spring, for he had been here many times before. His attention was drawn to the cages beside the tiny adobes. Fashioned from mesquite trunks and larger limbs, the crudely built wooden prisons held only a few naked Indian slaves. Iron Horse allowed himself a thin-lipped grin. Gold Tooth needed many *tarches* now, slaves for the silver mines down in Chihuahua and Coahuila. He would be eager to trade for more Apache captives. Iron Horse would soon have the repeating rifles he needed.

Mexican pistoleros in broad-brimmed sombreros watched Iron Horse and his warriors ride into the camp, rifles slung loosely in their hands, bearded faces shadowed by drooping hat brims. Iron Horse felt their stares, his muscles tensed for a betrayal. Only the direst of circumstances could have forced him to ride in plain sight before the muzzles of the Comancheros' guns. He knew Mexicans were not trustworthy, certainly not men who rode with Diente Oro. Valdez was himself a cow thief, wanted by the soldiers on both sides of the big river, and he would slit a man's throat for the boots he was wearing or the horse he rode. But Iron Horse knew that he and his followers were without choices. More soldiers were coming to the bluecoat fort in the mountains, and larger patrols now roamed far and wide, seeking him. Repeating rifles gave one warrior the strength of seven, for the mysterious guns somehow fired seven bullets before reloading was needed. Iron Horse knew he must have those rifles, and many bullets, before his war with the Tosi Tivo soldiers continued.

He led his warriors past one of the cages and glanced at the four scrawny Indians huddled inside the wooden bars. Diente Oro was starving his slaves into submission before loading them into the carts that would take them into Mexico.

Starving men gave less trouble and made fewer attempts to escape. Iron Horse smiled inwardly. Gold Tooth was as wise as the Great Owl.

At the largest adobe a figure came to the shaded doorway to stare at Iron Horse. A pair of pistols adorned his waist, catching shafts of slanted sunlight. Iron Horse watched Diente Oro closely as he kneed his pony toward the hut. If the Comanchero chieftain meant to betray him, he would be the first to die.

Iron Horse halted his pinto a few yards from the adobe, sitting silently, motionless. Valdez understood Comanche custom. He would allow an appropriate silence before he spoke, so the Four Spirits could hear the words between them and judge what was in the heart of each man.

Gold Tooth stepped out in the sunlight. Iron Horse stared into the Comanchero's eyes, seeking the truth behind his words before he talked. Iron Horse, without his spirit shield, would be able to see what was hidden inside Valdez's black heart.

"Welcome, Iron Horse," Diente Oro said. His voice was like the growl of an angry black bear.

Iron Horse grunted. He would speak to the Comanchero chieftain in the white man's tongue, though he knew only a few of the words and some were hard to say. "No *tarches*," he began in his own deep, guttural tone, sweeping a hand across the half-empty cages in the canyon. "We bring *tarches*. Trade for guns-shoot-many-bullets. Iron Horse need many-shoot guns." He watched Diente Oro's face, awaiting an answer.

The barrel-chested Mexican spread his palms. A crooked grin widened his thick black beard, revealing the gleaming gold tooth. "I have repeating rifles, Iron Horse," the Mexican said. "You bring me twenty strong *Indios* and I will give you ten Winchester rifles."

Iron Horse heard Diente Oro's words, and his hooded eyes revealed nothing, no hint of betrayal. But twenty Apache men would be hard to find and capture, and he was running out of time. "Ten *tarches* for ten many-shoot rifles." he said.

"Apaches go far to the west to hide from the bluecoats. We need guns now!"

Valdez took a step closer to Iron Horse's pony. Thick muscles rippled in his bare chest and arms. Iron Horse knew he would be a deadly adversary in a battle using only bare hands, or knives.

"You strike a hard bargain, Iron Horse," Valdez whispered hoarsely, making the sound of the hissing rattlesnake. His eyelids became slits and his grin faded.

Iron Horse returned the Comanchero's fierce glare. He would kill Diente Oro if he tried to trick him. Iron Horse had no fear of any man on the face of Mother Earth. "Ten *tarches*, ten guns," he said, as every muscle in his body tightened with smoldering anger.

Their eyes were locked together as if in mortal combat. Neither man would look away. The warriors behind Iron Horse sensed their war leader's building fury. Coppery fingers closed around the rifles they carried, preparing for the moment when Iron Horse shouted for the killing to begin.

Diente Oro was first to turn his head. He pointed to the closest group of Indian prisoners. "I must have slaves," he said. "The *patróns* who work the mines in the Sierra Madres grow impatient. I have only these few. See how poor they are?"

Iron Horse examined the cowering Apaches squatting inside the mesquite cage. Excrement had dried on their bare arms and legs, for there was no place without it where they could rest. Swarms of black flies hovered above the piles of droppings, making a buzzing noise. The starving prisoners made no effort to drive the flies from their filthy bodies, for the size of the task made it useless. Some of the prisoners were little more than skin and bones. They stared at Iron Horse with sunken, dead eyes, for they understood what fate awaited them in the mines of Mexico.

"I bring you ten strong Apaches," Iron Horse said. His tone left no doubt that it was his final offer. "Ten many-shoot guns and many bullets."

Diente Oro nodded once. "Then we have a bargain. Get down from your pony. We will drink a bottle of Boisa Pah."

Iron Horse grunted. He saw no treachery in Diente Oro's eyes.

The sleepy little town of Lajitas sat on the banks of the Rio Grande beneath a blistering August sun. Like most frontier Texas outposts, the citizenry kept up a constant vigilance against Indian attack and the forays of border bandits. The twenty-three residents of Lajitas were the first to face the murderous wrath of Iron Horse's renegade Comanche band when they acquired Winchester rifles.

Iron Horse struck with blinding speed and typical Kwahadie savagery an hour before sundown. Screaming warriors seemed to come from nowhere, before anyone in Lajitas could reach their guns. A blacksmith was the first to die, running from his forge toward his house. Homer Cathorn's head exploded in mid-stride when a .44 rimfire shell entered his right ear and came out the back of his skull. He collapsed on the caliche hardpan with a strangled cry and skidded along on his face and chest, but the rattle of rapid gunfire drowned out the sound as unshod ponies thundered into Lajitas.

Manuel Delgado died trying to reach his wife and children, from a bullet that shattered his spine. He fell in the road in front of the Lajitas Trading Post, owned by Addison Squires. Ad Squires came running out on the front porch of his store with a shotgun, only to be cut down by a bullet through his cheek that splattered blood and brains across the adobe wall behind him. As he crumpled to the porch, a speeding slug tore through his abdomen. His body jerked with false life, for he died the instant his skull ruptured.

Shrieking women and children ran for cover wherever they could find it, only to be hunted down by Iron Horse and his brutal killers and then shot. Guns cracked and banged all over Lajitas for less than three deadly minutes. Then an eerie silence fell. Now and then a rifle popped among the little adobe dwellings, or someone would scream. A pall of blue gun smoke hung above the settlement, for today, curiously, there was no dry West Texas wind. An ominous stillness had come to Lajitas only moments before the attack, as if the Great Spirit of the Comanches were holding his breath.

When the last living resident of the village uttered a final cry, Iron Horse and four warriors began looting Ad Squires's store, taking paper cartons of bullets and Colt pistols that fired brass-jacketed cartridges. Six mules taken from the livery were loaded with the guns, ammunition, and foodstuffs. Only when the packing was completed atop the mules did Iron Horse begin his inspection of the tasks he had assigned to the rest of his warriors.

He walked among the dead bodies around Lajitas, to examine the ritual mutilation of the white corpses. Grown men and women had been scalped and disemboweled, their intestines scattered around them like bloody, dust-encrusted rope. Male genitals were severed and placed in the victims' mouths. Womens' breasts were cut off, to make ammunition pouches after the skin was cured and dried. Good spirit medicine followed a warrior who carried his bullets in the pouches made from an enemy's breast. And Iron Horse knew, even with repeating guns, that he and his men would need good medicine for the forthcoming battles against the bluecoats.

Children of either sex were scalped. The curious yellow hair of some Tosi Tivo females was particularly prized. Iron Horse walked methodically through the drying blood, leaving his footprints in the pale white caliche dust, often mingled with crimson. The mutilations were necessary so the Tosi Tivo soldiers would read and understand the Comanche signature they were leaving behind. The bluecoats must know this slaughter was the handiwork of Iron Horse, for now they would also know that he had many-shoot guns.

Iron Horse came to the body of a young woman sprawled lifelessly beside an adobe hut. She was pretty, if white women could be called pretty. Somehow, she had been overlooked by the scalping knives. He kicked her with the toe of his deerskin boot and heard a groan. Slowly, his lips parted across his teeth in a wicked smile.

He bent down, seized her long yellow hair and began to

drag her away from the hut. The girl started to scream. When Iron Horse glanced over his shoulder, he saw her feet kicking. A cruel laugh burst forth from his throat. The girl would satisfy him and his men before she died.

He dragged her, kicking and screaming, to the road running through the middle of town, where he threw her head violently to the ground. From all across the village his warriors came toward him, drawn by the woman's screams.

The leering Kotsoteka asked to take her first, using sign language to ask his question. Iron Horse silenced him with a wicked lash with the back of his hand, then he unfastened the belt atop his leggings and knelt to grab the girl's knees, pulling them apart, laughing at her feeble struggle to keep him away.

One final death scream echoed across Lajitas before the last warrior mounted his pony. The naked girl's cry was garbled by the knife blade slashing across her throat. Iron Horse swung his pony away and heeled it to a lazy trot. Nine mounted men and six loaded pack mules followed him northward, toward the Christmas Mountains, leaving a trail of bloody droplets fallen from the scalp locks of every last man, woman, and child who had called Lajitas home.

The first cavalry patrol to reach Lajitas after the massacre followed the trail of blood for several miles. Then suddenly, as if the Comanches had sprouted wings, their tracks and the blood simply disappeared.

The United States Cavalry at Fort Davis combed the territory for the raiders for two months and came up with nothing. Even with Kickapoo scouts they found no tracks. Newspapers across the middle of Texas printed repeated demands that renegade Indian activity on the western frontier be stopped. A hue and cry reached the governor's office by the end of September, and as in the past, Governor Davis summoned Major Charlie Peoples of the state's foremost peacekeeping force, the Texas Rangers.

The governor of Texas issued a strange ultimatum when Major Peoples arrived: dispatch the deadliest guns in the service of the Rangers to far western Texas with orders to kill, until every renegade Comanche and gun-dealing Comanchero was wiped from the face of the earth.

Charlie Peoples wore a grim look when he left the governor's office that day, keeping several thoughts to himself as he hurried to mount his horse. It was nearing election time, and the governor wanted a public problem out of the way that might hinder his reelection.

Charlie knew just the right men for the job. A wire had to be sent to San Antonio, to Captain Will Dobbs. Charlie didn't know much about the renegade Indian problem out in West Texas, where they might be hiding, or how well they were armed. But he was sure of one thing—his solution. When the four rough-cut men of Company C got to the Davis Mountain region, there would be bloodshed aplenty, more than enough to satisfy the governor.

Charlie mounted his horse and swung toward the telegraph office down Congress Street. He shook his head, thinking about what he was about to do. Whoever the renegade Comanche leader might be, he was soon to face four of the toughest fighting men ever to wear a badge. Those renegades won't survive it, Charlie told himself. He could almost smell the blood in the air on a westerly wind as he trotted his horse to the telegraph office.

Chapter
Two

William Lee Dobbs had seen all he ever cared to
see of army posts and soldiers; the war had shown him
enough of that, those years of hardship and death with Gen-
eral John Bell Hood. In the years since, he had avoided con-
tacts with the military like the plague, although there were
times in the line of duty when it couldn't be escaped, when
cooperation was required between the Rangers and Federal
forces. Thus he sat in front of Major Ranald Copeland's desk
at Fort Davis, filled with misgivings. In most cases military
bureaucracy got in the way when he was in a hurry to get
things done.

"It's empty country down there, Captain," the major said,
rheumy eyes fixed on Will. "Our patrols have crisscrossed
that border region and can't come up with a thing. Three
good Kickapoo scouts haven't been able to find a track . . .
not a single track anywhere."

"One of my Rangers is a decent tracker, Major," Will
replied, wishing the talk would end. Protocol demanded that
they report to Major Copeland before they launched the manhunt for the Comanche raiders.

The major made a face. "Those men outside are a sorry-
looking lot," he said, without hiding his disgust. "If you ask
me, they look like common outlaws. Gunslingers. I wouldn't
sleep a wink with those three owlhoots in close proximity."

Will let out an impatient sigh. The conversation was going
nowhere, merely humoring the major's contempt for men
who didn't wear a uniform. "They've got some rough edges,
I'll admit," Will answered tiredly, glancing out an office

window. Through the smudgy pane of glass, he could see Carl Tumlinson slouched against a porch post, and he was forced to admit that Carl presented a rather ominous appearance among gentler folk. Carl was a thick-set hulk of a man who always wore a pugnacious expression. His demeanor wasn't helped any by the sawed-off, ten-gauge Greener shotgun dangling from a shoulder strap near his left hand, or the low-slung Colt .44 holstered against his right leg. Today he sported a week's worth of dark beard stubble which did nothing to enhance his looks. Will kept it a closely guarded secret that, to some extent, he agreed with Major Copeland's observation: Carl, and the others in Company C, might be hard to distinguish from the lawless element they were sworn to bring to justice. Years of experience as a Texas Ranger along the Texas-Mexican border had taught Will that the job required hard men, men who were just as tough and quick with a gun as the lawbreakers they tried to control.

"Just looking at them, Captain, I'd say they've got more than a few rough edges," the major insisted. The remark awakened Will's bad temper, a gift from his father, or so his mother always claimed. Will tried to control it, but now the major was poking his nose into affairs that were not his.

"They get the job done," Will said evenly. "Same thing can't always be said about the cavalry. You've had two months to track down those renegades, and the governor wants some action. We'll find them. May take a spell, but when we do, they'll go back to Austin in irons, or in a pine box."

Major Copeland gave Will a haughty glare. "You sound mighty damn sure of yourself," he snapped, bringing Will to the edge of his chair. "I wouldn't count on those misfits you've got to get this problem out of the governor's way. If I were wearing your boots, I'd be worried about getting a bullet in the back from one of my own men. Your men have no discipline, Captain. They won't follow orders when the chips are down. I've commanded fighting men for a number of years, and those men outside simply are not dependable. If they were, they would show some discipline, and take more pride in their appearance."

Will got up slowly, clamping his jaw, working the muscles in his cheeks. He placed his flat-brim hat atop his head and gave the major a level stare. "Those three men are among the best Rangers ever to wear the badge," he said, fighting his swelling rage. "We'll get the job done, and then you can explain to your superiors why the U.S. Army wandered all over this part of the state without finding anything. Put that in your report, Major—that your well-disciplined soldiers in their fancy blue uniforms couldn't do what four Texas Rangers got done."

Will wheeled for the office door and stalked out without waiting for the major's reply. A gust of wind swept past the front porch as Will closed the door behind him. For a moment he stood, his gaunt frame outlined inside the canvas duster flapping about his legs, while he gazed across the fort compound. Then his eyes wandered to the three Rangers resting against the hitch rail in front of the building. Billy Blue was watching Will's face, reading his expression in the shadow beneath his drooping hat brim. Leon Graves's hawk-like face was aimed at Will. Only Carl was otherwise occupied, midway through a huge swallow of whiskey from the pint bottle in his fist. Carl believed that a drink of whiskey befit any occasion.

"Let's ride," Will growled, seething over the upstart major's remarks. He stepped off the shaded porch and mounted his long-muscled dun gelding.

The four Rangers trotted their horses toward the gates out of Fort Davis. Their faces were hidden by low-pulled hat brims, each shrouded by a long-tailed duster coat. Soldiers all over the compound stopped to stare at them, some pausing to notice the heavy armament booted to the Rangers' saddles, and the bulge of pistols inside their coats. Winchester rifles and shotguns adorned each saddle. Wooden canteens and bulky saddlebags jostled with the horses' gait. They rode past a pair of sentries and swung due south outside the wall.

Major Copeland watched the four men depart into the heat haze with a frown pinching his features. "Damn bunch of paid guns is all they are," he muttered. "They won't find anything down there," he added softly. "Maybe a Comanche bullet, or a scalping knife when they lose their hair."

He remembered, with dislike, the Ranger captain's hard face, his handlebar mustache. "I'd bet he was wanted by the law himself someplace," he said, sure of the judgment. "Damn Confederate." He turned for his office door and dismissed the notion that Rangers could find the renegade gang in the empty mountains and canyons south of the fort, or the elusive Comanchero gunrunners who supplied them. Eighty seasoned cavalrymen led by experienced Indian scouts couldn't find them. Most certainly, four saloon gunmen wearing tin badges stood no chance of succeeding. They'd be dead, or back in Austin by the end of the month.

Billy Blue stared thoughtfully at the distant mountains. Will trusted Billy's instincts when it came to hunting men. Billy had been a bounty hunter for a decade after the war and he knew his business, the nature of men on the run.

"Tell me what the major said about the guns," he said. "Where do the Indians get them?"

Will frowned. Major Copeland had given him only bits and pieces of information, and given it grudgingly. "They're called Comancheros," he said after a moment of recollection. "For years the same bunch has crossed back an' forth from Mexico, trading guns and ammunition to the Comanches. Used to be raw gold and silver they were after. The Kotsoteka band knew where some of the old Spanish mines were hidden, and they'd trade ore for what they needed. A Comanche don't have any use for metal . . . don't know how to melt it down. Copeland said the Comanchero leader was a half-breed called Diente Oro Valdez. Means Gold Tooth in *español*."

Leon Graves spoke up when he heard the name. "He's just another dogshit Mexican, Cap'n. I'll dig that gold tooth out of his mouth, soon as I kill him. Everybody can call him Gap Tooth after that, after I bust that gold outta his jaw."

Will shook his head. Leon's penchant for killing Mexicans

was well established at Ranger headquarters. Major Peoples had been called to task for the oversupply of spilled blood that time down in Encinal, when Company C battled a gang of Mexican revolutionaries over a wagonload of contraband guns. The governor had wanted to know why Will's report listed forty-eight Mexican casualties, the bulk being credited to Ranger Leon Graves. Leon had gone on a killing spree when the Mexicans attacked Encinal. He was a dead shot with a rifle and did not stop firing until the last member of Zambrano's gang went down; then he calmly walked among the wounded and killed them at close range. It was then that Will fully understood the imbalance in Leon's brain. He enjoyed killing, and took satisfaction in it when his victims were Mexicans. Something half cocked inside Leon's skull went off as soon as a fight started. Leon was the loose cannon on the deck of Will's ship, a man he was barely able to control when there was violence.

But when Company C faced long odds, as they often did, there was no better man to have siding with the Rangers than Leon. Will had been forced to accept Leon's faults, given the job they were asked to do along the Rio Grande. Men with good sense wouldn't take the job in the first place.

"Finding those Comancheros is the place to start," Billy said after a moment of contemplation. "Them Comanches won't be far away, needin' bullets for their guns. When a man goes huntin' rattlesnakes, he'll find 'em where there's food. Iron Horse can't get what he's after without ammunition. We find Gold Tooth Valdez, an' we'll find Iron Horse close by."

"Makes sense," Will replied, squinting in the sunlight to view the mountains looming before them. "Valdez will be close to the border, so he can jump back across if the law gets close. A Comanche ain't civilized enough to understand how a river can make a man safe. To him it's just a river. I say we ride down the Rio Grande and look for fresh tracks. Maybe they'll belong to Diente Oro."

Carl took a bubbling swallow of whiskey and then smacked his lips. "This is mighty dry country, Cap'n," he offered needlessly. "Even a goddamn Injun has gotta have water. If we can find any springs in them mountains, that'll be a good place to look. Me an' little Betsy here are damn sure ready to start killin' Comanches." He patted the stock of his ten-gauge and grinned. "Ain't never got the chance to kill a redskin yet. Kinda lookin' forward to it . . . see if they die same as a white man."

"Prettiest sight on earth is a dead Mexican," Leon remarked, as if he were talking about a change in the weather.

Will tried to put Leon's observation out of his mind so he could form a sensible plan. Listening to Leon and Carl talk about killing was a waste of time. Both men were fearless and seemed to enjoy a deadly confrontation. Only Billy showed the good sense to approach a fight with caution.

To Will's disappointment, Carl was in a surly mood and wouldn't let the subject drop. "A dead Injun might be just as pretty, Leon," Carl argued. "Times, it's hard to tell what a feller looked like when Betsy gets done with him. If there ain't no skin left on his bones, a man can't tell what color or breed he was to start with. Me, I ain't all that damn particular 'bout who I shoot, an' you oughta do the same. Just kill the son of a bitch if he needs killin' and stop worryin' about his family tree."

Will noticed the grin on Billy's face just then.

"These two are itchin' for a fight, Cap'n," Billy said. "Best we hurry up and find 'em somethin' to shoot at or they'll start tryin' to kill each other."

Will took a deep breath and nodded once. "Let's hurry these horses some," he said, touching a spur rowel to the dun's ribs, asking the gelding for a lope. A winding switchback led south away from Fort Davis, to a flat thick with ocotillo and beds of cactus. According to the major, there wasn't much flat country in the hundred-mile ride to reach the river, and Will meant to make good time over what little level ground there was.

Galloping south under a late-day sun, Will considered what lay in store. They were riding into unfamiliar country. The surveyor's map in his saddlebags revealed almost nothing about the hundreds of square miles of canyons and mountains above the border. This region was the last unsettled frontier in Texas, said to be as wild as any part of the state ever was. It was land that would never be tamed by the plow, far too dry and rocky for cultivation, and thus unclaimed by westward expansion. This was a last haven for renegade Comanches and Apaches, those few who refused to sign the treaties that sent tribes to government-owned reservations farther north and east. Little towns like Lajitas and Presidio sprang up along the river, where small farmers could find water for their meager crops. Twenty-three settlers had given up their lives at Lajitas in such a quest. Down deep, Will knew more would come, as soon as the memory of the massacre faded. It was left to men like Will and the Rangers of Company C to police the widely scattered settlements in the farthest reaches of Texas. It was an impossible job, given the distances, the isolation. Only after a bloody slaughter, like the one in Lajitas, was any focus given to a particular trouble spot. There were far too many other lawless places across the state for an undermanned force of Rangers.

Will's dun lengthened its strides across the ocotillo flat as the sun lowered to the west. He was leading his men toward a one-sided fight in the emptiest part of Texas, and the deeper they rode into the barren mountains, the more his doubts grew. They were up against a band of the most savage people on earth—the Comanches. An unknown number of renegades had struck tiny Lajitas. Could just four Rangers handle such a task?

No sense worryin' about it now, he told himself, reining his horse wide of a cholla plant. The time to worry is when we find them. Or when they find us.

Dust curled away from their horses' heels, sending a telltale warning into the sky that someone was entering the northern edge of the Santiago range. Farther south they would strike the Christmas Mountains, said to be even drier, more formidable. A hundred miles of hostile land stretched to the river, land they would have to comb very carefully for faint hoofprints, always staying within range of precious water for their horses, constantly on the alert for an ambush by Iron Horse. Over the years, Will had been handed some tough assignments, but never anything with so many uncertainties as this mandate handed down from the governor's office. It was his nature to accept the most difficult jobs, and accomplish them if he could. But there was something about this manhunt that seemed overwhelming, next to impossible. The size of the region, and its emptiness, warned of futility.

Later, as they started up the next rocky hills south of the flat, he tried to reason things out and put his worries to rest. Billy could read tracks like some men read a newspaper. If and when any shooting started, Will knew he was accompanied by three men who knew their trade. Two of his Rangers would actually enjoy the contest with Iron Horse and Gold Tooth Valdez, as if it were all a deadly game.

Chapter
Three

Billy knelt beside a piece of barren caliche, peering down at faint impressions in the pale earth. A dry wind howled through the empty village of Lajitas, kicking up swirls of dust. Will watched Billy intently while the Ranger tried to glean the smallest scrap of information from the hoofprints. Billy's shoulder-length brown hair fluttered around his face below the crown of his sweat-stained hat.

"Too old, Cap'n," Billy muttered, tracing a fingertip over the lip of one shallow print. "Wasn't shod horses, so it's a safe bet they were Indian ponies. Been too long. This damn wind is near 'bout as bad as rain when it comes to wipin' out tracks."

Will swung a glance to the graves behind the trading post. A few crude wooden markers bore names of the dead. Others simply read, FEMALE. ABOUT 14, or WHITE WOMAN. SCALPED, and MEXICAN CHILD. The graveyard was a black reminder of the raid led by Iron Horse. Major Copeland had described what his soldiers found when they first came to the blood-soaked ground. The massacre had occured in August, and now it was October. Looking for the renegades' tracks was a waste of time, and the soldiers' footprints had obliterated the truth of what had happened here when the burial detail went about its gruesome chore. Lajitas was only a place to start the search for Iron Horse and the Comancheros who supplied him. It was a beginning, since they hadn't found any tracks in the Santiagos, or the Christmas range, on the ride down to the border.

Will aimed a look south, to the Rio Grande. A muddy

brown current flowed between the banks, forming slow eddies around hidden sandbars here and there, moving syrup-like toward the distant gulf. Beyond the river lay Mexico, a haven for all manner of outlaws and cutthroats who sought escape from the law. Upriver, on the Mexican side, sat the lawless pueblo Ojinaga, where a blind man could toss a rock in any direction with long odds that the rock would strike a man wanted in Texas, or beyond.

Billy stood up and tilted his hat brim to see Will's face. "No use, Cap'n," he said. "They rode north. That's all these tracks have to tell."

The Christmas Mountains, through which they had come to reach the river, lay to the north, dry and forbidding. Billy had found nothing along the rocky pathways through the range, not a hoofprint or so much as a scratch that might have marked the passage of a barefoot Indian pony.

Will sighed. "Let's ride down the river," he said. He was bone tired, and so were his men, after pushing through the mountains to reach Lajitas before a rain wiped out every trace of the raid. Fall rains were long overdue, and only this morning a bank of clouds had formed along the southwestern horizon.

"We're near 'bout out of whiskey, Cap'n," Carl observed with an edge creeping into his voice. Without his daily supply of whiskey, Carl's disposition turned ugly. Of almost equal concern, Carl would complain about his thirst until more whiskey could be found. Everyone's ears would ring with endless strings of cussing until Carl's saddlebags bulged with pint bottles. Even rotgut satisfied Carl when he was on the prod for a drink. He wasn't picky about women or liquor, or much of anything else.

"You drank it all up," Leon suggested, sounding disgusted. "I never saw a feller who could drink so much red-eye and not fall plumb off his horse. Feel sorry for that roan horse of yours, havin' to tote so much whiskey around."

Carl wasn't in the mood for good-natured needling right then. He looked at Leon and his eyes narrowed. "It was hot, an' I'm thirsty when it gets hot," he growled.

Leon gave Carl a one-sided grin. He had a prominent Adam's apple that bobbed up and down when he spoke. "You ever hear of water, Carl?" he asked. "Ride with me down to that river an' I'll introduce you to it, afore that rotgut eats a hole plumb through your belly so all your insides fall out."

Carl's eyelids slitted even more. "I'll take you down there an' drown you if'n you don't tend to your own affairs. If I take the notion, I'll bring along a whole wagonload of whiskey. Who asked you for your goddamn opinion anyway?"

Leon merely shrugged and looked away, ending the argument. They were friends, but when Carl's nerves were raw, Leon knew just how far Carl could be pushed. Will had sometimes wondered who would win a battle between them. The winner would have to make sure the other was dead to be certain of his victory. Both men were crazy when it came to facing death. Neither one had ever shown the slightest concern for his own safety when lead was whistling through the air.

Billy mounted his dust-caked bay and gave the ground a final examination. "Let's head down that river," he said, touching his horse with a spur.

They trotted their mounts down to the banks of the Rio Grande so the horses could drink their fill. Will scanned the bluffs on the Mexican side while the animals drank, thinking about what the screams and gun blasts must have sounded like echoing off the cliffs the day Iron Horse rode into Lajitas. Will knew what it was like to fight Comanches back in wilder times, when the Kwahadies and Kotsotekas sizzled the Llano country with their murderous forays. As a rookie Ranger his first assignment had been to Fort Mason, where he'd been taught firsthand what it was like to battle men who were only fleeting shadows among the live oak trees. Fighting Yankees had been easy, put beside a war with the Comanches. He'd almost lost his life at Fort Mason back in '69, and the memory of it still haunted his slumber now and then.

Will was distracted from his ruminations by the sound of a cork pulled from the neck of a bottle. He looked at Carl, knowing he was the source of the sound. Carl tilted a half-empty pint to his lips and drank a generous swallow, then sighed contentedly.

"Best medicine there is," Carl announced. "Don't know what the hell I'm gonna do when I run out of medicine."

Leon's throaty chuckle sounded above the rattle of horseshoes as they reined away. "Medicine's for sick folks, Carl," he said, grinning. "You ain't never been sick a day in your life that I remember. Maybe that's because you're always too damn drunk to take notice. That horse piss you're drinkin' ain't medicine. Fact is, it'd kill a man who didn't have iron insides. One of these days you'll be ridin' along an' your belly is gonna fall in your lap an' then I can bury you. I'll use a whiskey bottle fer a grave marker. That way everybody'll know who's buried there . . . won't need to worry 'bout spellin' your name right."

Carl glanced at Leon, then his face softened and he shrugged his powerful shoulders. "I'd like that," he said thoughtfully, casting an eye to the sky, "only I'd ask that you put a full jug in the box before you cover me up . . . just in case I wake up an' want a drink to pass the time."

Will tried to ignore the banter, making a study of the ground for fresh tracks as they left Lajitas behind. Finding hoofprints was Billy's job, but it was better than listening to Carl and Leon talk foolishness, so Will focused his attention on the sandy soil beside the Rio Grande. Somewhere along the river, they would find evidence of a recent crossing. The gun traders supplying Iron Horse had to enter Mexico with whatever the renegades bartered for guns and ammunition. The gun dealers were men, and men left tracks. Only a clever Comanche could defy the rule, in Will's experience.

"Yonder's an offshoot canyon," Billy remarked, pointing to a distant opening in the cliff beside the river. "Let's ride up and see what we find. It's gonna take a spell to check every one of these openings, but I can't figure no other way to be sure we've covered every inch of this river."

Will sighed and settled against the cantle of his saddle. "If you say so, Billy," he answered softly, scanning the opening. "Our orders say to find these owlhoots. That wire from Charlie said not to head back till we had prisoners. Or dead bodies."

"I'll promise you some corpses, Cap'n," Leon said. "All Billy's got to do is show us where the sumbitches are, an' I'll do the rest."

Before Will could reply, Carl spoke.

"Like hell you will," he growled, making a face. "Me an' little Betsy are gonna get our share. I didn't come this far to be a damn spectator. I'm wagerin' a month's pay I kill more of the sons of bitches than ol' Leon, on accounta I ain't so damn particular 'bout what breed I shoot."

Will closed his mind to the discussion and reined in behind Billy to ride toward the mouth of the feeder canyon, wondering if they would ever find a target for their guns. He could never have imagined a country so vast, so completely empty. Adding to the feeling of emptiness was the absolute silence around them. The clatter of their horses' hooves rolled like thunder off the canyon walls, as if the sound did not belong here.

A mesquite knot popped in the fire, sending a shower of tiny sparks into the night sky. Somewhere high on the rim of the river canyon, a coyote howled mournfully at the stars. Will shivered inside his thin canvas duster and glanced toward the sound, palming a tin cup of coffee for its warmth. A chill had come to the canyon with nightfall, reminding him that it was late October, time for the harsh blue northers to sweep down from the high plains of Llano Estacado as fall became winter. They had plenty of blankets and provisions, but when a cold North Texas wind commenced, they would suffer.

"That coyote sounds mighty lonesome," Carl remarked absently, staring at the flames. "This is damn sure the lonesomest place I ever saw, so it figures that coyote's got a right to complain."

Leon was pacing back and forth just outside the circle of firelight, staring off into the night. It was Leon's nature to be edgy when they were riding into a fight. Curiously, when the fighting started, he appeared calm. "They're out there someplace," Leon said in a faraway voice. "I get this feelin' when there's somebody out there watchin'. Got that feelin' real strong just now."

Carl inclined his head toward Leon. "He's just plain scared," Carl said, wearing a sardonic grin. "Ain't no such thing as a feelin' when somebody's lookin' at you. Eyeballs ain't got no feel. It's a damn aggravation, havin' to put up with all his superstitious ways. We'd all be better off if somebody'd cut out his tongue."

"Somebody's out there," Leon flatly. "When one of them sneaky redskins gives you a haircut tonight while you're tryin' to sleep, you remember I told you they was close. It'll save you the price of a barber shop anyways, Carl. Be just what you deserve."

Will listened to the sounds of Leon's boots, wondering if Leon could be right. Was Iron Horse watching them now? Maybe from the cliffs above? These mountains and canyons belonged to his renegade band, and he would know every back trail, every hiding place. Would he also know when intruders entered his domain? Had he been watching them ever since they rode through the Santiagos?

"That wasn't a coyote," Billy said in a voice that was almost a whisper. "It was a signal."

Will's face turned sharply to Billy. "How can you be sure?" he asked.

The others were watching Billy before he gave his answer. Billy allowed a moment of silence before he spoke.

"A coyote barks four times before it howls," he said. "That cry we heard had five barks. I counted 'em real careful. I 'spect that was Iron Horse, tellin' the rest of his bunch that we're here."

Leon had stopped pacing. Carl's eyelids were mere slits when he heard what Billy had to say. Will lifted his gaze to the dark cliffs above their camp and moved his eyes slowly along the rim.

"You right sure 'bout that?" Carl asked hoarsely, fixing Billy with a stare.

Billy nodded once. "Learned it from an old Kiowa horse

thief a long time ago,'' Billy replied. ''Kiowas were the best horse thieves back then. When them Kiowas circled a herd of horses, they called to each other like a coyote . . . only they added an extra bark, so the others would know where they were. That damn sure wasn't a coyote we just heard. That was an Injun.''

Carl's meaty fist closed around the stock of his Greener as his head swiveled around the darkness. ''Let 'em come,'' he snarled. ''I'm almost out of whiskey anyway. It'd suit me just fine if we got this over with . . . before my throat gets dry.''

Leon stood rock-still at the edge of the firelight. Cords of ropelike muscle stood out in his neck, and his cheeks worked with agitation. Will noticed that Leon had begun to blink furiously, a nervous tic he developed when he felt the nearness of a fight.

''I could use a drink of that rotgut myself just now, Carl,'' he said quietly. ''Pass me that bottle a'fore you drink it plumb dry.''

Will got up, still watching the inky shadows along the rim above them. ''I'll sleep better with my rifle close by,'' he said, turning toward the saddles piled behind him. ''Leon, find a place where you can keep an eye on our horses. And check their hobbles every now an' then. A man on foot out here is the same as dead. From here on we keep our mounts real close. I'll relieve you in a couple of hours, after a little shut-eye.''

Billy stood up and dusted off the seat of his pants. ''No sense in gettin' worried just yet, Cap'n,'' he said. ''When they decide to come after us or our broncs, they'll be real quiet when they get in rifle range. Long as we can hear 'em, we're safe.''

Despite Billy's assurances, Will felt a growing uneasiness. He drew his Winchester from its saddle boot and cradled it in the crook of his arm while he spread his bedroll. When he levered a shell into the firing chamber and lowered the hammer with his thumb, the men around the fire turned toward the sound. Resting his head against the seat of his saddle, he placed his hat over his face, wondering if he'd be able to sleep at all.

Minutes later, after Leon's footfalls moved off in the direction of the horses, a faint cry echoed from the west. Every muscle in Will's body stiffened as he counted the yipping barks before the eerie howl.

"That was five," he heard Carl say.

Will hadn't needed any help with the tally. When the fifth bark sounded in the distance, tiny hairs stood up on the back of his neck, and his mouth felt uncommonly dry. He knew enough about fighting Comanches to fear them. If he slept at all tonight, his dreams would be frightening things, recollections of those early days at Fort Mason when mounted apparitions swept past the fort walls, screaming their savage war cries, firing rifles with deadly accuracy at Rangers huddled behind meager barricades of loose-piled stone. Not even the terrible Confederate defeat at Franklin, Tennessee, could compare to those months of struggle to hold Fort Mason against endless Comanche assaults. At Franklin there had been a place to run, a line of retreat. Encircled by screaming Kwahadies at Fort Mason, all the Rangers could do was fight. Or die in the attempt.

Carl's boots made a heavy sound when they carried his weight away from the fire. Will lifted his hat brim with a thumb and found Billy alone beside the campfire.

"Havin' trouble drifting off, Cap'n?" Billy asked when he glanced over to Will.

"Some," Will answered softly. "Lots of old memories when it comes to fightin' Comanches. They're hard bastards to kill."

Billy grunted and shook his head. "Iron Horse will be smart," he said thoughtfully. "He's been givin' the army the slip for quite a spell. These ain't gonna be the easiest orders to follow, Will. A man could make a strong case for sendin' more'n four Rangers to get this done."

Will lowered his hat brim and closed his eyes. "Try tellin' that to Charlie Peoples," he replied. "The way he figures things, all it takes is just one Ranger to handle trouble. Any more is a waste of men who could be doin' something else."

Chapter
Four

Will tented his shoulders, palms resting atop his saddle horn. A week of fruitless search along the Rio Grande had worn away at his nerves. Every sound, even the slightest movement, made him jumpy now. He'd slept little at night, listening for the coyote calls, and when he did sleep, he dreamed about Horace Biggs and that terror-filled moment back in the summer of '69 when a Comanche scalping knife sliced off a plug of the younger Ranger's hair. Before Will could load his rifle, the screaming Kwahadie had vanished. Lying behind a low rock wall, all Will could do was grip his rifle stock and listen to the dying Ranger's shrill cries beyond the barricade, until they finally ended when blood loss claimed Horace. Will knew he would never forget those pain-ridden screams, or the agonizing hour before they stopped. During that time, Will had come to know a part of himself that somehow remained hidden during four long years of fighting Yankees. He had come face-to-face with overpowering fear which kept him frozen behind a pile of rocks while a fellow Ranger died. He'd been unable to force his limbs to move, as if he were imprisoned inside a block of ice. After that day he understood the real meaning of fear in a way he'd never been able to grasp before. A dark side of his own nature had been revealed to him—he wasn't the fearless soldier he thought he was—and the realization numbed him for weeks after the Comanche attack.

Now, he watched Billy ride slow circles up the mouth of another offshoot canyon, scanning the ground as he covered the width of the opening. It did not seem possible that there were no tracks anywhere they looked. Seven days riding southeast of Lajitas and they'd found nothing, not a single hoofprint.

"We're wastin' our goddamn time," Carl grumbled. "I say the yellow bastards cleared out for Mexico. If I carried any knittin' needles in my saddlebags, I'd start makin' myself a pair of socks. There ain't any goddamn Injuns down here, Cap'n. Maybe them folks back at Lajitas died from the pox, an' the buzzards chewed up the bodies, so it'd look like redskins done it."

Will didn't bother to answer. Carl had been out of whiskey for two days, and nothing short of a full-fledged war would satisfy him. Or a barrel of whiskey.

"Did you hear what I said, Cap'n?" Carl persisted, scowling as he looked at Will.

Will aimed an angry stare toward Carl. Carl was pushing him and he wouldn't tolerate it, not in the mood he found himself in. "When I want your opinion, I'll ask for it," he snapped, boring into Carl with a look. "Until then, keep it to yourself. I don't give a damn what you think, Ranger. I'm drawin' the captain's pay around here, in case you forgot."

For a fleeting moment Will saw the challenge in Carl's green eyes, then the smoldering fire faded and his expression was blank. Will shook his head and turned his gaze absently in another direction, but the muscles in his cheeks remained tight. Carl had never evidenced any fear of another man, and Will wondered if a time would come when Carl refused an order, daring him to force his hand. Carl would be a dangerous adversary. Mere fractions of a second would determine who would live and who would die. Commanding men such as Carl was never an easy job. Men of his ilk were always a half step away from going off like a powder keg, sometimes in the wrong direction. Keeping him under control required an iron hand, much the same as the tight rein he tried to keep on Leon.

Billy trotted his horse back to the river. He shrugged as he drew his bay to a halt, waiting for a cloud of caliche dust

to settle around his horse before he spoke. "Nothin',
Cap'n," he said tiredly. "Javelina tracks and a few deer.
Been a week an' we ain't found any sign down here."

"Keep lookin'," Will growled, gritting his teeth around
the words as he looked downriver. "Those bastards are here
someplace, and I aim to find 'em."

Leon hawked up a ball of phlegm and spat below a stirrup.
"I say we split up, Cap'n," he said. "Cover more ground
that way."

Will wagged his head side to side. "That's just what Iron
Horse wants us to do. Be easier to kill us, one at a time."

"The yellow sumbitch has hightailed it fer Mexico," Carl
said with heat in his voice. "We ain't never gonna find him,
'cause he ain't here."

Will ended the discussion by touching a spur to his horse.
The dun struck a dog trot beside the river, snorting dust from
its muzzle as it carried Will farther south into the canyon
marked Santa Elena on the surveyor's map. Few landmarks
had names on the piece of paper folded in his saddlebags, as
though no one found the mountains and canyons worthy of
identification. For a time Will listened to the squeak of saddle
leather and the rattle of the dun's bit, the click of horseshoes
against rock. He could never remember being so tired. Perhaps tonight he'd be able to sleep.

Half an hour later Billy rode to the entrance of another
narrow feeder canyon. Will watched idly, his mind at rest,
until he saw Billy swing down from his horse to kneel above
a spot between the towering canyon walls.

Then Billy gave a sharp whistle, bringing Will full awake.

"Over here!" Billy shouted, waving a palm above his
head.

Will hurried his dun to the opening and swung down before the gelding came to a stop. Billy was pointing down.

At first Will saw nothing but caliche and clumps of dry
bunch grass, until his eyes came to rest on an unusual marking in the dust. Following the impression into the niche, he
recognized a wagon track leading up the canyon. "How old
is it?" he asked softly.

"Mighty recent," Billy answered, touching the print tenderly with a fingertip. "No more'n a couple of days. Wagon wasn't loaded very heavy. Pulled by a burro, these little hoofprints here between the wheels. Could be only a Mexican with a load of clay pots or a cart full of corn."

Will shook his head against Billy's guess. "Not way out here. No place to go with a load of anything . . . 'cept maybe a load of guns and ammunition for Iron Horse. These tracks are gonna take us to that Comanchero camp, Billy. I can feel it in my bones."

Billy let out a ragged breath and stood up, squinting into the mouth of the niche. "Wherever they take us, we'd best ride real slow an' careful. We could get our heads shot off from most anyplace up on those cliffs. A bushwhacker'd have an easy time of it, up there."

Will tilted his head skyward to view the rim. "Maybe we oughta find a way up there ourselves," he said thoughtfully. "No sense ridin' into a trap. See if you can find a way to the top, Billy. Even if one of us has to climb up there on foot, we can't just ride blind up that passage."

"I'll go, Cap'n," Leon said, sitting his horse a few yards away. "I can take a rifle up yonder and make damn sure the way is clear of Injuns or Mexicans before the rest of you ride in."

"Leon's the best shot with a Winchester," Carl added, agreeing with Leon's plan quickly. "He can pick a sand fly off a buzzard's snout from up there."

Will examined the climb to reach the rim. Sheer walls of stone reached hundreds of feet high above the river. A man would have a hard time finding his way to the top, but when he did, the men in the passageway would have some protection from a dry gulcher. "See if you can climb up," he said after a moment of contemplation. "Take plenty of shells, and make damn sure you stay out of sight while you clear the way for us an' the horses."

Leon was out of his saddle before Will could finish his remarks. Shedding his duster, he tied it behind his bedroll and began to pocket cartridges for his Winchester. Will no-

ticed a satisfied grin tugging the corners of Leon's mouth.
Leon sensed the nearness of a battle and it obviously pleased
him.

Leon withdrew the rifle from its saddle boot and levered
a shell into the firing chamber. He glanced up at Will. "I'll
give a wave when I git to the top," he said, then he wheeled
for the rock wall behind him and trotted toward it, shoulder-
ing his Winchester, swiveling his head to find the easiest
place to climb.

Will walked to his dun and climbed stiffly into the saddle,
with a lingering look into the passage where they would ride.
Billy mounted and swung his bay toward the opening, then
halted the gelding and stared silently at the niche.

The click of a gun metal behind Will distracted him. When
he glanced over his shoulder, he saw Carl examining the
loads in his shotgun before closing the breech.

"Wanted to make damn sure Betsy's ready to tear into
some meat," Carl growled savagely, jutting his square jaw.
Then his pale eyes flickered over the canyon mouth, his lips
drawn in a thin line. "I could goddamn sure use a drink right
about now," he added. "Had the shakes so bad last night I
hardly got any sleep. If there's anybody up that draw yonder,
they'd better be ready fer some hot lead soon as I get there,
'cause I'm damn sure in a hurry to head back where there's
whiskey."

Billy shook his head, giving Carl a mirthless grin. "Make
damn sure of your aim before that cannon goes off," he said
quietly. "If I had some candle wax, I'd stick plugs in my ears.
I'll be deaf as a fence post if I ride alongside you much longer,
Carl. Thunder is quieter than that scattergun you carry."

Will swung a look to Leon's progress up the canyon
wall. The lanky Ranger somehow found tiny footholds in
the rock, inching higher toward a ledge that would take
him to the rim. Will's dun stamped a hoof impatiently at
a fly. For a minute more there was absolute silence while
the three Rangers watched Leon scale the slab of stone to
reach the ledge, clinging to his rifle up a seemingly impossible climb.

Leon stood up and waved to the others, then he hurried along the ledge and went out of sight behind a rocky outcrop.

"I swear that feller's part mountain goat," Carl said absently. "The other part is crazy as a sackful of loons for tryin' it in the first place. He figures he's gonna get a chance to shoot Meskins. Otherwise, he'd be sittin' right here on his horse."

"It's the truth that he ain't none too fond of gents who talk Spanish," Billy said. "When he was a boy—maybe eight or nine—he saw his paw gunned down by a gang of *bandidos*, then they tied his maw to a four-poster bed an' made him watch while they used her. Ol' Leon ain't never got over it. He told me about it one time, when he was drunk as a hoot owl on tequila. He hates a Meskin worse'n a preacher hates sin. I tried to explain that there was good Meskins as well as bad, but he wasn't listnin' to a word I said. He still remembers what they done to his maw an' paw."

Carl grunted, watching the rim. "I'd say it's might' near impossible to get a new idea into Leon's skullbone. Hardheadedest gent I ever saw. The claim could be made that Leon's dumb. A chicken's got more sense sometimes. But he's damn sure a good feller to have sidin' with you when the shootin' starts. He's a dead shot with that rifle he's carryin', that's fer sure."

"Worst is, he likes it," Billy added with a frown. "I've tried to talk to him about it. Same as talkin' to a stump."

"Let's ride," Will said, urging his dun forward. Talking about Leon's penchant for killing had gotten on his nerves. If he was any judge of things, Leon would have ample opportunity to vent some of his blood lust in the days ahead. Iron Horse wouldn't give up peacefully. Neither would the gun merchant known as Gold Tooth Valdez, facing a stretch in jail, or a short drop from a hangman's gallows if the governor was in a bad humor.

The dun plodded into the opening at the front of the line of Rangers, until Billy swung past Will at a trot to scour the ground for more tracks. The wagon sign plainly marked the direction up the passage. No one had tried to hide the impressions made by the wheels.

Will glanced up, a quarter mile into the canyon. For a time he saw nothing, until Leon's shadow fell across a rock along the edge of the rim. "Slow down, Billy," Will warned. "Let Leon have some time to get farther ahead of us."

An anxious hour passed for Will, walking his horse deeper into the niche, then halting until Leon waved down at them that the way was clear. A knot had formed in Will's belly. Near a bend in the tightening canyon he opened the front of his duster, tucked the tail behind the butt of his Colt .44, and lifted the hammer thong for a fast pull. Noticing that Billy had taken his Winchester from the boot below his leg, Will did the same, chambering a shell needlessly, ejecting a fresh load to the dirt beneath his horse, which he hardly seemed to notice. The closeness of the walls around them made him jittery. The clatter of shod horses bounced off the rocks, making enough noise to wake the dead, in Will's view. He was only dimly aware that his palms were sweating and that his hat band seemed tight as Billy started around the bend in the passage. A faint drumming sound reached Will's ears; he recognized it as the beating of his heart.

Billy rode out of sight behind a jumble of boulders fallen from the rim. Then, suddenly, a rifle barked above the passage, spooking Will's horse.

He heard Billy's horse wheel around and lunge into a run. In the blink of an eye Billy's bay rounded the turn at a hard gallop with Billy lying flat over its withers. Another gunshot sounded from the far side of the canyon top, then two more in rapid succession, bearing Leon's signature.

A scream echoed off the rocks somewhere in front of them, a cry of pain. Before the cry ended, Carl came spurring past Will at a headlong run, pounding his spurs into the roan's sides with his shotgun leveled in front of him. Will opened his mouth to shout a warning, knowing it was too late—the first shot had been fired in a gunfight, signaling something inside Carl's brain that it was time to act, no matter what the risk.

Chapter
Five

The Greener gave off its ear-splitting roar beyond the turn. The canyon walls seemed to convulse when they contained the sound. Will was left without choices. One of his men had ridden into gunfire around the bend, and the others must back his play. He drove spurs into the dun and shouldered his Winchester when the horse bounded to a gallop. Before the thunderous echo of the shotgun blast died away, Will's dun carried him around the turn to face whatever lay in store.

A shallow basin widened the passage in front of him, and in the fleeting seconds he had, Will saw scattered adobe huts across the basin floor. Guns began to crack and pop from the shadows below stunted trees around the basin; he glimpsed muzzle flashes and tiny puffs of gun smoke curling away from half a dozen spots.

Carl's shotgun exploded, deafening Will to the chatter of other guns. Will saw Carl's roan gelding shy away from the boiling load of buckshot screaming above its ears, its strides faltering briefly, until it felt the punishment of Carl's spurs again, clanking relentlessly against its flanks. Will couldn't find a target in the deep shadows, though Carl apparently had less trouble. Carl's head was turned toward one of the adobes, and when he saw the body of a man tumble to the ground in front of the open doorway, he raised his Greener above his head and cried, "Got the son of a bitch!"

A speeding bullet sizzled above Will's head while the dun charged into the melee. Another slug whispered near Will's cheek, and he ducked away reflexively, still forcing his horse

to an all-out run into the basin, without anything to shoot at
beyond flickering fingers of orange flame and billowing gun
smoke.

A movement along one canyon wall caught his eye—a
Mexican in a broad-brimmed sombrero ran for a split-rail
corral behind one of the huts. Will raised his Winchester and
thumbed back the hammer, trying to steady his sights amid
the jolts of the dun's bounding gait. In a split second, briefly
frozen in time, his rifle muzzle came to rest on the running
man and he squeezed the trigger. The Winchester slammed
into Will's shoulder like the kick of a mule, spitting out its
life-stopping load with a bone-jarring thud that hurt his ears.

The Mexican's legs halted in mid-stride—he seemed sus-
pended in the air for too long a time, then his torso careened
into the cliff beside him when the force of the slug drove him
against the rock. A splatter of crimson caught sunlight behind him, glistening wetly as he slid down the rock face to
his rump. His sombrero toppled to the ground beside him,
fluttering like a wounded bird. Will chambered another cartridge when the banging of guns returned to his ringing ears,
his horse racing among the adobes now, carrying him into a
deadly cross fire from the scattered groves of mesquites
across the canyon floor.

Rifle fire pounded from the rim above Will's head, seven
shots coming so quickly it seemed impossible that they came
from a single gun. But above the din Will told himself who
was firing down into the basin. Leon was exacting a terrible
price in blood from high atop the west wall.

The dun reached the side of an adobe hut, where Will
jerked the gelding to a sliding halt. Guns cracked and popped
from every direction while bullets whined through the air, so
many sounds that they became a single noise in the heat of
pitched battle. His dun shied when a slug ricocheted off the
adobe, tilting Will dangerously in the saddle until he caught
himself with the saddle horn. Then he glimpsed a man in the
shadows of a nearby thicket of mesquites. Whirling, he
brought the Winchester to bear on the man's outline and trig-
gered a hasty shot at the trees.

Will's target was lifted off the ground when the slug struck, then torn sideways, arms windmilling, feet flailing before falling out of sight in the purple shadows. As Will levered a shell into the firing chamber, the ground seemed to move underneath his dun and a mighty roar shook the basin, blotting out every other sound.

"Got the son of a bitch!" he heard Carl cry, almost before the roar faded.

The clatter of galloping horses reached Will. At the north end of the basin men and horses were moving inside a cloud of pale dust. Sombreroed riders were bent low, firing pistols in Will's direction from the backs of lunging animals. Will saw a lone rider charging after them and recognized Billy, aiming round after round toward the escaping Mexicans. One man flew from his saddle as if he'd sprouted wings, arms outstretched before he fell out of sight in the dust behind the horses. Four mounted men disappeared into a slice in the rock. Billy was far too cautious to charge headlong after them. He jerked his gelding to a bounding stop near the spot where the riders went up the passage.

Will swung his dun away from the adobe wall. The gunfire had died down to an occasional pop. Leon's rifle fell silent up on the rim, and for a time there was an eerie quiet.

Then Carl's Greener erupted with a bellowing blast near one of the huts. Will's horse snorted and bowed its neck when the noise startled it so suddenly. Carl's announcement claiming another victim was lost in the chatter of gunfire from above when Leon poured three rapid shots into the canyon.

Billy's horse came galloping toward Will, iron shoes clattering over rocky soil. Billy hauled back on his reins when the bay reached the adobe, bringing the animal to a sliding halt.

The silence returned to the basin. Acrid gun smoke stung Will's nostrils, and there was a hint of coppery blood in the air. From the corner of his eye, Will saw Carl jump from the back of his roan near one of the huts.

"Four of 'em rode clear up that draw, Cap'n," Billy said,

taking Will's attention from Carl. "You want us to go after 'em?"

Scanning his surroundings, Will took a deep breath. "Not just yet," he answered in a hoarse whisper. "Let's make damn sure the rest of them are out of it." He glanced up at the rim and waved Leon down, finally relaxing his grip on his rifle stock.

Only then did he really notice the crude wooden cages close to the huts, puzzling over the arrangement of so many pointed stakes bound together to form walls. A closer look at one of the squares revealed a few bronze-skinned captives huddled in a far corner. Coal-black hair framed the faces of the prisoners. Two more cages held small groups of naked men, cowering in a shadow cast below the adobes. "They're holding Indian captives," Will remarked softly, unable to guess the purpose behind it.

A sound drew Will's attention away from the Indians inside the wooden bars. Heavy boots clumped toward him, a barrel-chested Mexican marching in front of the shotgun Carl rested against his spine. A crooked grin lifted one corner of Carl's mouth as he prodded his prisoner with the gun muzzles. The big Mexican's hands were raised above his head, jutting higher quickly when he felt a nudge against his backbone.

"Got one of the bastards alive," Carl said, and Will could hear the disappointment in Carl's voice. "Yellow sumbitch throwed out his guns an' put his hands up so I couldn't blow his head off. If you remember, I told you these sumbitches was yellow, Cap'n. Killin' the rest of 'em is gonna be easy."

Carl halted his captive near Will's left stirrup. Now that the shooting had stopped, Will could direct his full attention to the Mexican Carl had captured.

"*Quien es?*" Will demanded, fixing the man with a cold stare.

"Santiago," the Mexican replied, his eyes bulging in their sockets when Carl poked his ribs with the Greener. "Santiago Cortez, senor."

"Habla inglés?" Will inquired, preferring to question the man in English.

"Sí . . . yes. A little," Cortez responded in thickly accented words. A pair of crisscrossed bandoliers adorned his broad chest, gleaming with brass-jacketed cartridges. When he spoke, his thick black beard parted, revealing yellowed, broken teeth at the front of his mouth. Clad in leather leggings and a dog-eared cloth vest, he had an unwashed appearance about him, as though he'd avoided bathwater whenever he could.

Will prepared a list of questions. "Why do you keep these Indians in the cages?" he began.

Cortez hesitated. "For the mines in Mexico," he answered in a slow, reluctant voice.

"How many men were camped here?" Will asked. "How many men ride for Diente Oro?"

The Mexican's eyes rounded with surprise, then his look hardened and Will knew he would try to hide the truth. "Who is . . . this Diente Oro, senor? I know of no one by that name."

Before Will could ask more, Carl swung around to Cortez's side with his lips drawn back in a snarl. "This Meskin sumbitch is lyin' to us, Cap'n," he snapped. Suddenly the twin muzzles of Carl's ten-gauge were buried in the soft flesh of Cortez's neck, partly hidden by untrimmed swirls of his beard. Carl cocked both hammers on his Greener, and the dual clicks were ominous sounds. "I'll just feed his goddamn brains to the sparrows!" Carl shouted, probing deeper into the Mexican's neck with the gun. "Give the order, Cap'n, an' I'll scatter this lyin' bastard's head—"

"Hold off, Carl!" Will cried, fearing that Carl would make good on the promise before they could learn more about Gold Tooth Valdez and Iron Horse. Their prisoner had valuable information. Killing him made no sense.

Cortez tried to back away from the pressure of Carl's shotgun while a string of words poured from his mouth. *"Sí, sí!"* he shrieked in a high-pitched voice. *"Esta Diente Oro!*

No kill me, senor! I will tell you everything, only *por favor*, spare my life!''

"Then start talkin'," Carl hissed. "And if you lie to the cap'n one more time, I swear I'll leave nothin' but a stump where your head used to be. An' quit jabberin' that goddamn Spanish, so I can understand what you're sayin'.''

Running feet came toward them from the west side of the basin, rattling spurs. Leon approached in a loop-legged run, cradling his Winchester in front of him. Will noticed a glassy look in his eyes when he reached them, out of breath.

"How come you didn't kill this one, Carl?" Leon asked, as if a live prisoner bewildered him. "How come you ain't shot him yet?"

Carl gave Leon an unhappy look. "The cap'n wants to ask him some questions, Leon. I done offered to blow his head off, but Cap'n Dobbs won't allow it.''

"How many men ride with Diente Oro?" Will asked again, to end the debate between Leon and Carl and get on with the questioning.

Cortez seemed to be counting silently, then said, "Fourteen," in a strangled tone, garbled by the shotgun against his throat.

"I killed three of the sumbitches," Carl said with unconcealed pride. "Was gonna make it four, only this yellow bastard—''

"Did Diente Oro get away?" Will interjected, silencing Carl.

Cortez tried to nod, though the gun prevented it. "*Si*, senor. He rode north. You will not find him, or the others. He knows this place like the back of his hand.''

"Where is Iron Horse?" Will continued. "Tell me the truth. Your life depends on it.''

"*Alla*," Cortez replied, aiming a thick finger northwest. "There is a secret place, a stronghold, in the mountains. Iron Horse has his lodges there, for the winter. Where two tall mountains are very close together, you will find the trail to the top." Cortez swallowed and looked askance. "He will kill you, senor," he said, speaking in a softer voice. "If you go there, Iron Horse will take your hair. Four men will have no chance against him. His warriors are *muy malo hombres*, and they have no fear.''

''We'll see about that,'' Leon remarked, fingers closing around his rifle. ''Maybe I'll be the one to take his hair off. It ain't been decided just yet who's gonna lose his scalp.''

Will let out a whispering breath of air, thinking. Keeping Santiago Cortez with them as a prisoner would only slow them down when they went looking for Valdez and Iron Horse. But what to do with him? He wouldn't allow Carl to kill him. Will's gaze drifted to one of the wooden cages, noting that the Indians inside were starving, little more than gaunt skeletons. ''Let's free those captives and put this gent in one of the cages. We can leave him a bucket of water and enough food for a week or two. He'll be here when we get back, so we can put him in irons an' take him back to Austin.''

''It'd be a hell of a lot easier to kill him,'' Leon protested, as if the notion of returning with a prisoner offended him in some senseless way. The fact that Cortez was a Mexican pushed Leon toward his solution.

The remark irritated Will. ''Have you forgotten about that badge you're wearin'?'' he asked hotly, making no effort to hide his anger. ''You aren't gettin' paid to execute every Mexican we run across, Ranger. You took an oath to uphold the law, and by God you'll keep that oath when you ride with Company C. Put this prisoner in one of the cages, an' give him some water and food. That's an order!''

''Yessir, Cap'n,'' Leon replied meekly, adopting a hangdog look. ''I was only sayin' it'd be easier to do it my way.''

Carl lowered his shotgun and gave Will a questioning look. ''No call to get all riled up, Cap'n,'' he said. ''Hell, this damn Meskin is a Comanchero gunrunner. It ain't like ol' Leon was talkin' about gunnin' down a village priest or a schoolteacher. This sorry sumbitch deserves to die, if you ask my opinion on it.''

''I *didn't* ask,'' Will growled. ''Put irons on this prisoner and toss him in a cage. I'm tired of arguing over it!''

Carl hung his head. "Yessir," he mumbled, then he raised his gun and aimed the barrels toward the closest wooden stockade. "Get movin'," he growled, shoving Cortez away from Will's horse.

Will ground his teeth together, turning to Billy. "Let's set the rest of those Indians free," he said, reining the dun in the direction of the cages. He spoke to Leon over his shoulder. "Get a count of the men we shot . . . and gather up any guns you can find."

"You mean we ain't goin' after the rest of 'em?" Leon asked, evidencing keen disappointment.

"We've got work to do here first," Will answered, urging his horse toward one of the wooden stockades.

It was then Will noticed a spring at the center of the canyon, encircled by slender cottonwoods. The location of the Comanchero hideout made more sense now. The tiny pool allowed Valdez to stay hidden here for as long as he wanted.

When he approached the cage, the scent of excrement wrinkled his nostrils. Swarms of black flies hovered over piles of human waste, buzzing faintly, moving in swirling clouds. Three scrawny Indians stared at Will and Billy until the horses halted. The sight, and the stench arising from the cage floor, turned Will's stomach.

"Kept 'em penned up like wild animals," Billy observed, swinging a leg over the rump of his bay to dismount. "Pitiful sight, ain't it?"

Will nodded and got down from his horse, examining a gate fashioned from thick mesquite limbs held in place by a length of rusted chain. A fist-sized padlock dangled where the links of chain were joined. "We'll need a key," he remarked absently, his attention on the prisoners now. Two naked men watched fearfully when Will walked to the gate, their sunken eyes fixed on his rifle. Their ribs jutted against thin coppery skin, bony arms and legs without flesh, reminding Will of the starving Yankee prisoners he saw at Andersonville in Georgia just before the end of the war. "They ain't Comanches," he said, for the men did not wear their shoulder-length hair in twin braids, Comanche-fashion.

"I'd guess they're Apaches. Whoever they are, they're damn near starved to death. We'll give 'em some food and turn 'em loose. Maybe they can find their own way back home, wherever they came from."

Billy was peering closely through the bars. "One of 'em's a girl, Cap'n," he said. "The one hidin' behind the others. Maybe we oughta get her some clothes . . . take some britches off one of them dead Comancheros, and a shirt. Look at her—she's a right pretty young thing, if she had a bath."

For the first time Will examined the slender Indian standing behind the two men. In spite of the flies clinging to her skin, and a black mane of matted hair, he found he was forced to agree with Billy. The young girl had a broad, pretty face with high cheekbones and big chocolate eyes, eyes that seemed dull with despair. Her small breasts were perfectly shaped, hanging down her thin rib cage, and she made no effort to cover herself. Will supposed Indians knew nothing about modesty. Or was she simply too frightened to care if the pair of white men stared at her nakedness?

"I'll poke around in the huts for the key," Will said quietly, without taking his eyes from the Indian girl. He discovered that he was strangely taken by her raw beauty, despite the filth caked to her body, and the flies. "See if you can round up somethin' for them to eat, Billy. Maybe Valdez kept a supply of jerky. . . ."

Chapter Six

He walked among the adobe huts, peering inside when he came to a door frame. The crude furnishings revealed nothing—one or two rawhide cots, hand-fashioned stools or an occasional chair, a plank table inside the larger hut where a bottle of mescal held a mere two fingers of amber liquid. On a peg above the table, Will found a rusted ring of keys. He saw leg irons and lengths of rusted chain piled in one corner. "For the prisoners," he muttered, taking down the keys. Then his gaze wandered to a bunk along the back wall and, underneath it, a newly milled pine box bearing an imprint: THE WINCHESTER REPEATING ARMS COMPANY.

He knelt and removed the lid on the shipping crate, only to find it empty. "The rifles Valdez traded to Iron Horse," he said, a dark frown pinching his features. "He's running slaves into Mexico he trades for Winchesters. Means those renegades are armed with repeaters. Damn the luck." He got up and tossed the lid aside, turning for the door. Beyond the opening he could see Leon dragging the body of a Comanchero across a sunlit stretch of ground. "What the hell. . . ?" he whispered. His scowl deepened as he came to the doorway.

Leon had begun a grisly monument to the Rangers' marksmanship in front of an adobe. Five bullet-torn bodies were sprawled on the caliche, arranged in a neat row. Blood smears in the dirt marked the passage of each corpse to its resting place. One Comanchero had only a pulpy mass for a face, plainly a victim of Carl's short-barrel shotgun at close range. Sighting Leon's fascination with this display of dead men brought bitter bile to Will's throat. Only a madman would find perverse pleasure in such a gruesome undertaking. Will knew it was pointless, however, trying to talk to Leon about the senselessness of what he was doing. Like a clock ticking badly, something that words could never fix was out of kilter inside Leon's head. When Leon turned around, Will saw that same odd, glassy look in his eyes. Leon's hands were covered with blood, though he hardly seemed to pay any heed, bent on the completion of his task.

Will swung around the door frame with the ring of keys, swallowing bile. Crossing the hardpan to the closest wooden cage, he put his mind on other things. From the corner of his eye he saw Billy emerge from one of the huts with an armload of dried sausages.

"This stuff ain't half bad," Billy said, his cheeks bulging with meat. "Hell of a lot of chili pepper in it."

Will fisted the padlock binding the chain around the gate and tried a key, then another, until tumblers gave way. Glancing inside to the captive Indians, his nose wrinkled involuntarily at the stench. Four gaunt-framed men watched him open the lock with fearful eyes, until the gate swung back on creaking rawhide hinges.

"Offer 'em some of that food," Will said, motioning for the men to come outside. Two Indians started toward Will when he gave the signal, moving forward on weakened legs, although their footsteps were hesitant, uncertain.

Billy held out a sausage. One captive took it quickly and stuffed the whole link into his mouth. Then the others crowded around Billy with extended palms. One Indian boy was so thin that Will could see every rib across his chest. He took the shriveled piece of sausage and simply stared at it for a time, then began to devour it.

Will turned for the next cage and started between the huts with old memories of Andersonville floating before his eyes. Thousands of men had starved to death there in the final months of the war, and among the terrible sights Will remembered, Andersonville was the worst. The leg irons and chains Valdez kept for his prisoners hardly seemed necessary, in Will's view. Men starved down to skin and bones made few attempts to escape, and they wouldn't run far.

Behind one of the adobes, Will noticed a two-wheeled cart with wooden sides like those around the cages. It was the conveyance used to carry the captive Indians into Mexico, he supposed. The tracks of those wagon wheels had led them to the Comanchero camp.

He opened another gate and stood back, motioning to three more starving men huddled in a corner of the stockade. The Indians had seen the others walk out to accept the meat from Billy, and when Will backed away from the opening, the three slender men crept out, giving Will a sideways glance. Will held his breath to keep out the smell until Billy came toward the freed prisoners, then he whirled away and allowed air into his lungs, batting flies from his face. He was stricken by the cruelty of what Valdez had done to the Indians as he strode toward the remaining cage, where the girl was kept. He did not need to be told what the Comancheros had done to the woman, for it was certain that they had used her. He saw her face peering at him from behind one of the men when he drew near the gate. She was, as Billy said and he himself had noted, a pretty young woman, and Will knew she would not have escaped the urges of fourteen hard-bitten men.

The smell of offal was overpowering as he opened the padlock. Flies swarmed around him until the chain was free. The gate opened with a crack. The men inside crept toward him, but the girl remained in a corner, staring numbly into his eyes.

"I won't hurt you," he said, knowing she wouldn't understand the words, hoping that his grin would reassure her. *"No molestar,"* he added in Spanish, waving her toward him. *"Comida para ti.* We've got food, and nobody'll harm you."

Her eyelids lowered, but she showed no sign of understanding what he said, standing rock-still at the back of the cage, refusing to come closer. The Indian men trotted away behind Will, hurrying over to Billy and the sausages.

"Bring me a piece of that meat," Will said over his shoulder. "The girl won't come out. She's scared of me. Maybe if I give her some food, she'll know we don't aim to hurt her. Fetch me a shirt, so she can cover herself. Try an' find one that ain't got any blood on it. . . . ."

Billy passed out sausages to the hungry men and brought a link to Will, but his gaze was fixed on the naked woman. "When she's cleaned up, she'll be damn near beautiful," he said softly. He stared at her breasts a moment longer, then swung away from the cage.

Will stood in the opening and held out the sausage. "It's okay," he said gently, grinning again. The girl seemed to be staring at his handlebar mustache, then she looked deeply into his eyes and moved the tip of her tongue across her sun-cracked lips. She was hungry, though she still did not trust the man who offered her food. Will guessed her doubts were the result of her experiences at the hands of Valdez and his pistoleros. When he looked at her more closely, he noticed a purple bruise on her left cheek.

Slowly the girl's hand moved to cover the mound of dark hair between her thighs. Then she shook her head back and forth, to say no.

Will nodded, to tell her that he understood. He took a step into the cage, extending the sausage to her. "Don't worry," he told her softly. "I ain't gonna touch you."

Flies swarmed away from his boots when he entered the cage, and the smell worsened. He wondered how anyone could have survived the stink for very long.

At first the girl drew back when he neared her, and now her dark eyes showed fear, widening. But when the piece of meat was within her grasp, a tiny hand flew out to seize it from his fingers.

"That's the idea," he said, backing away a half step. "Eat it. You're safe now. Those men are gone. You're free to go."

He heard Billy's footfalls behind him, and turned to see Billy with a homespun cotton shirt draped over his forearm. The shirt was deeply soiled and sweat-stained, but it would cover the girl.

He took the garment from Billy and approached the woman again while she was chewing the sausage. This time she did not draw back when he was close. She took the shirt and swallowed, then snaked her arms into the sleeves and closed the front, clasping it tightly with her fingers.

Will motioned her to the gate and walked outside, taking a huge breath of fresher air when he was away from the smell and the flies. The girl came hesitantly behind him, pausing between strides to watch Will's face, then coming forward again. She took another bite of meat when she was free of the prison, and it seemed she almost smiled. Her eyes wandered to the spring hidden in the shadows of the cottonwood trees, and she pointed to it, as if asking permission for a drink.

Will nodded. "Go anyplace you want, little lady," he said.

She whirled and trotted off toward the pool, glancing over her shoulder, perhaps to see if Will or Billy would follow. The hem of her shirt barely covered the swell of her buttocks when she ran, a fact both Will and Billy noticed until she went out of sight in the shadows.

"That makes eleven of them, countin' the girl," Billy said. "Some of 'em look mighty pitiful, thin as they are. A few'll have trouble makin' it very far if they have to walk. There's a pair of mules back yonder in a corral. Maybe we oughta let 'em have those mules, for the ones too weak to walk."

"Good idea," Will sighed, turning away from the spring. "We'll pick four of the best animals for ourselves an' let the Indians have the rest. No tellin' how far they've got to go—"

A whoop inside one of the adobes swung Will around. It was Carl who yelled as he came out of the hut, and he wore a broad grin. A full bottle of mescal decorated his right fist. He held it aloft, showing it to the others.

"Medicine!" he cried, then pulled the cork with his teeth and spat it over his shoulder. Carl drank thirstily and made a face, drawing his shirtsleeve across his lips. "Ya'll come over an' have a drink," he added. "Tastes like liquid fire, but it's good for what ails you."

Santiago Cortez was seated on the ground outside the adobe, his wrists and ankles bound with irons. He glowered at Carl when he saw the bottle and looked away.

Will heard the faint splash of water inside the cottonwood grove and turned toward the sound. Outlined in the shade below the limbs, he saw the girl washing herself. The shirt hung from a branch at the water's edge. "Looks like you're gonna get your wish, Billy," he reflected. "She's gettin' cleaned up. Sure as hell wish the others would, so we'd be rid of that damned smell. . . ."

Billy was otherwise distracted for the moment, handing out more sausages to the Indian men crowded around him. Will noticed then how small the freed prisoners seemed alongside Billy. Most Indians were short-statured, the ones Will had seen. But not the Comanche. Comanche men were tall, imposing figures with hawk-beak noses, and when they rode a mustang pony, they became like a part of the horse, as though they'd grown to the animal's back. Mounted Comanches made a fearsome sight among men who knew how skillfully they waged war.

Spurs rattled to Will's right. Leon came trudging out of a mesquite thicket dragging another limp body by the heels. In spite of himself, Will watched the dead Comanchero's head bounce lifelessly over the ground, arms trailing. "He's gone plumb loco this time," Will said to himself. But he had not made the remark softly enough to prevent Leon from hearing him.

"I'm leavin' ol' Gold Tooth a message, Cap'n," Leon explained, hauling the corpse past Will toward the row of bodies. "This way, he'll know we mean business if he comes back to his hideout. When he sees his compadres laid out in front of his doorstep, he'll know this wasn't just a social call."

Will ground his teeth together and shook his head, certain that he would never understand how Leon's brain worked. He looked away from the trail of blood behind Leon, determined to push it from his mind.

Billy chuckled. "What's the matter, Cap'n? You look kinda

pale just now," he said, as if enjoying Will's unhappy reaction to what Leon was doing.

"Don't hardly seem necessary," Will complained.

Billy handed out the last sausage and walked over to Will, his expression serious now. "Leon has his faults," Billy said quietly. "I'll admit he's soft in the head 'bout some things. But to my way of thinkin', a feller's got to remember why the major sent us down here in the first place. Twenty-three innocent settlers got killed and scalped back yonder at Lajitas. Some of 'em was little kids, hardly more'n walking age. These Meskin gunrunners gave Iron Horse what he needed to slaughter those folks . . . an' look what this bunch done to these Injuns. The army couldn't put a stop to it, couldn't even find Valdez or Iron Horse, so I say it's okay by me to turn a feller like Leon Graves loose amongst 'em. This ain't an honorable war, Cap'n. The men we're after are savages, cold-blooded killers who'll do anything to get what they want. You gotta fight men like that with whatever it takes to get the job done. In my estimation, that makes Leon and Carl the perfect men for the job."

Will looked up at the canyon rim, thinking about what Billy said. "You're right," he replied a moment later. "This sure as hell ain't no honorable fight, an' the odds are long against us. If the four of us had any sense, we'd turn in our badges and find easier work."

Billy clapped Will on the shoulder. "Don't pay no attention to Leon," he said softly. "Him'n Carl will carry their share of the load when the chips are down."

A clatter ended Will's ruminations. Carl was tossing the dead men's guns in a heap near the row of corpses. Pistols, rifles, and shotguns caught sunlight amid the pile of weaponry. The bottle of mescal sat in the shade below the roof of the adobe, helping Will to a decision that a drink might soften his mood. He jammed his hands in the pockets of his duster and walked over to the hut, determined not to look at Leon's handiwork along the way. When he picked up the mescal, he knew Cortez was watching him. The Comanchero's sullen expression did not change as Will sent a bubbling swallow of liquor down his throat.

"Diente Oro will kill you all," Cortez hissed, rattling the irons around his wrists, doubling his fists. "You will pay for what you have done here, senor. The coyotes will scatter your bones, *pendejos*!"

The threat caught Will at the wrong time, unleashing his temper before he thought to control it. His right hand clawed the Walker free of its holster. He swung the gun barrel to Cortez and stalked over to the seated Comanchero. Cortez opened his mouth to cry out, and in that same instant Will jammed the muzzle of his .44 in the Mexican's mouth, forcing it back against his tongue.

"Maybe," Will whispered savagely, cocking the gun. "But just before that happens, I can promise you a hole through your skullbone big enough to make the wind howl! If you talk to Gold Tooth before I get back, tell him I'm lookin' for him! Be sure you tell him that!"

Cortez's eyes had begun to blink furiously; he tried to talk, but the words were muffled by cold iron. Then the muscles in Will's gun hand relaxed when he fought to control himself.

"You shoulda let me kill him, Cap'n," he heard Leon say. "If those Comancheros come back while we're lookin' for Iron Horse, they'll turn him loose an' we'll have to try to kill him all over again. If we shoot him, he won't be shootin' at us."

"Lemme blow his goddamn head off!" Carl shouted, running from a spot behind the adobe. "He was mine in the first place," Carl protested, with genuine hurt in his voice, clanking his spurs to reach Will before Will did the job himself.

Will took a deep breath and removed the gun from Cortez's lips as his sudden anger subsided. Will sighed heavily, holstering his gun. "We ain't gonna shoot him. It'll be up to a judge to decide what happens to him."

Will swung away from Cortez, sighting north. "Pick out four of the best horses in that corral an' string 'em together. Time we got movin', after we set fire to that pile of guns.

We'll leave the rest of the horses and mules for these Indians. Some of 'em ain't hardly strong enough to walk.'' He remembered the girl, and looked toward the spring. ''Fetch me a gentle horse for the woman,'' he added. ''If we can make 'em understand, they can ride with us till we're out of this canyon.''

He started for the pool, with the intention of tossing the ring of keys to the bottom after Cortez was safely locked in one of the cages. He glimpsed the girl sleeving into the shirt Billy gave her, wondering if she would run away when he entered the trees. A gust of wind ruffled the duster about his legs, but he was thinking about the woman now.

Chapter Seven

The sounds of his spurs startled her. She had been kneeling at the edge of the pool, combing through her damp hair with her fingers while she looked at her reflection on the glassy surface. But when she heard his approach, she jumped to her feet and backed away, closing the front of the shirt.

He grinned at her when he entered the shaded ground beneath the cottonwoods, hoping to ease her fears. Reminded of his manners, even though the girl was an Indian who would never understand a white man's ways, he pulled off his hat and spoke to her. "I won't hurt you," he said gently. "I'll just throw these keys to the bottom and be on my way. One of my men is gettin' a horse for you to ride. You can go back to your people now . . . whenever you're ready."

He took the ring of keys from a pocket of his duster and tossed it into the depths of the pool. A splash rippled the surface, forming tiny circles that spread away from the spot. The girl watched him closely, but this time she wore a softer expression. Will raised a hand, beckoning for her to follow him. "That horse," he said, and added *"caballo"* in the event she understood a little Spanish.

He noticed that her arms and legs were clean now, still damp from her bath. And with her hair freshly washed, she was indeed a beautiful woman. The shirt clung to her damp skin, outlining every curve of her body. In spite of himself, Will felt a warm sensation spread through his groin.

"Come with me," he said, barely a whisper, smiling to reassure her.

51

For a moment longer she remained frozen to the spot at the edge of the pool. Then she took a small, tentative step in his direction, and then another. Her eyes searched his face, but now there was no fear in them. A hint of doubt, perhaps, as she came closer, almost within reach.

"I'm not gonna hurt you," he said again. If she could not grasp his meaning, she might trust the tone of his voice.

The girl halted in front of him, and he saw a question on her face. "Eat," she said, and at first he couldn't be sure he'd heard her correctly.

"We've got more food in our saddlebags," he told her. "We'll give you more to eat, and a horse to ride. Do you understand?"

She nodded silently, and it surprised him.

"Where did you learn English?" he asked.

"English?"

Will shook his head. "The white man's tongue," he answered carefully, speaking slowly.

"Padres," she replied. It was the Spanish name for a priest, though she said it strangely, with a curious accent.

"Habla español?" he continued, to determine if she spoke more Spanish than English, if her schooling had come from a priest.

She wagged her head side to side slowly, pointing to herself. "Lipan," she said, stabbing her chest with a finger. "I Lipan. No talk padre talk. White man talk. Some." She pinched her thumb and finger together; to indicate a small amount, perhaps.

"Come," he said, waving her closer. "You can eat, and I'll get you that horse I promised."

A trace of a smile lifted the corners of her mouth, though it faded quickly. Then she lowered a hand and covered her genitals again and shook her head. "No," she whispered. There was hurt in her eyes when she said it.

Will nodded that he understood. "No. None of that. No one will touch you . . . down there, or anyplace else. You've got my word."

He turned away from the pool and started out of the trees,

looking back, motioning for her to follow. She came slowly behind, clutching the front of the shirt, until they walked out in bright sunlight. Will led the way toward his dun, to take strips of jerky from his saddlebags. Now and then he glanced back, making sure the girl was behind him.

The Indian men stood in a group near a stand of mesquites, and all eyes were on Will and the woman as he led her to his horse. The men seemed uncertain what to do now, free of the cages. Will opened a saddlebag and handed the girl strips of dried meat. She took them but kept her distance, still suspicious of him.

He watched her take a bite of jerky, admiring the roundness of her hips inside the damp shirttail clinging to her like a second skin. Then he examined her face again; her aquiline nose, which seemed to fit the rest of her features; her eyes, reminding him of dark pools, strangely bottomless. Few Indian women he had seen could equal her remarkable beauty, and the same might be said about the white women he'd known.

Billy came from the corral, leading a rawboned brown mare with a slash Y branded on its left shoulder. The mare was probably stolen during one of Valdez's forays into Texas. Saddle marks on its withers attested that it was broken to ride. Billy walked up to the Lipan girl and handed her the reins.

"This old mare's gentle," he said to Will. "There's three burros and that pair of mules we can leave the men. Picked out four geldings we can use for spares. Not much to look at, most of 'em, but they're sound on all four feet an' shod all 'round with good iron. Got 'em tied to the fence yonder. If you can figure a way to tell them Injuns they can have the rest—"

"The girl speaks a little English," Will offered. He turned to the woman. "Take the mules and burros," he said, pointing to the corral, "for the men who are too weak to walk."

The girl inclined her head, as though she understood, her cheeks still bulging with jerky. She held the mare's reins, but her gaze never left Will's face.

The sounds of a scuffle sent him whirling around, only to find Carl standing over Santiago Cortez near the gate into one of the cages. Cortez was sprawled on his face, trying to scramble to his feet while hampered by his manacles.

Carl noticed the look Will sent in his direction. "The sumbitch made a grab for my six-gun, Cap'n," Carl protested. "Had to swat him over the head to get his attention. Said he didn't wanna go in there with all that Injun shit, but I reckon he will now, with that lump on his skull." Carl raised a boot to the seat of Cortez's pants and kicked him in the rump. The blow sent Cortez forward into the cage, where he landed on his face and chest.

Carl shut the gate and fastened the padlock. Then he gave his prisoner a leer. "You'll know how them Injuns felt in a day or two," he growled.

Leon had assumed what Will would call a proud pose at the feet of the dead Comancheros, resting his blood-soaked hands on his hips, admiring the neatness of the row. "Pile some brush around those guns and set fire to it," Will commanded. "Then get mounted and bring those extra horses. We're pullin' outta here to look for Iron Horse."

"Iron . . . Horse," the girl said haltingly. She was pointing northwest when Will looked at her.

"Where?" Will asked. "Do you know where he is?"

She shook her head, still pointing in the same direction.

"Can you take us there?" Will continued. "There's a place where two mountains are close together . . ."

The girl nodded again and walked to the mare's withers, then swung gracefully over the brown's back. Her right hand made some sort of sign, wiggling, and at first Will did not understand.

"That's the sign of a snake crawling backward," Billy said. "It's the sign all Injuns use to describe Comanches. Most every tribe talks the same sign talk, an' that's damn sure the sign they use to say that they've seen Comanches."

"Then she understands who we're after," Will said. "If she'll show us where those two mountains are, we can do the rest."

The girl swung her mare toward the slice in the north canyon wall. She said something to the rest of the Indian prisoners and pointed to the corral. The tongue she spoke was guttural, words that were impossible to understand. But the men seemed to know what she wanted—they started toward the mules and burros, whispering among themselves.

Billy hurried away to halter the spare mounts while Will gave Leon a hand piling brittle brush over the pile of weapons. Without needing instructions from Will, Carl gathered their canteens from each saddle and headed for the spring to fill them, still clinging to the half-drunk mescal bottle, sipping from it now and then.

Will turned to the woman when the brush smoldered from a match to dry tinder. She sat the mare, watching Will without expression. At the corral, the freed prisoners were haltering mules and donkeys. Billy led four multibranded geldings from the corral gate, more stolen livestock, judging by the different brands. Billy tied the lead rope on the first gelding to his saddle horn, then mounted his bay and cast a look at the flames licking higher in the brush pile. Carl was hurrying back from the spring before Will mounted. Leon had already climbed aboard his bay, holding the reins on Carl's roan.

Will gave the Comanchero hideout a final look after he stepped in a stirrup and mounted his dun. His gaze lingered on the cage where Santiago Cortez pressed his face to the wooden bars. Carl had placed a pail of water inside the gate and a few strips of jerky. Will decided there was no harm in leaving Cortez to the fates. If he lost a little weight before he was freed, he'd be none the worse for it. And there was a chance he might gain some understanding of what he'd done to the starving Indians.

Will reined over to the girl and halted his horse when their knees were almost touching. "How far?" he asked. "How far to the camp of Iron Horse?"

Her features pinched with thought while she gazed northwest in silence. Then she said, "Four suns. Come," and her heels thumped against the mare's ribs to lead the way.

Four suns, Will thought glumly. Four days of hard riding in this wasteland. He looked over his shoulder and waved the other Rangers onward, thinking black thoughts now that he knew the distance before them. The sun was already slanted to the west, and dark would come soon. More trouble might be lurking for them then. Gold Tooth Valdez and three of his henchmen were out there somewhere with revenge for a motive. And now the Lipan girl was taking them in the same direction Valdez had ridden only hours before, up the narrow passageway through solid rock. Valdez might easily ambush them; he would know all the right places. Hadn't Santiago Cortez said that Diente Oro knew these canyons like the back of his hand?

They followed the girl into the mouth of the niche at a walk, and Will was filled with misgivings when the cliffs closed in around them. From above Valdez would have an easy time of it, firing down at the procession of Rangers. Sweat formed on Will's brow, trickling down his face. He felt a growing certainty that they were making a stupid move, riding blind up the twisting passage. To calm his fears the best he could, he pulled his Winchester and rested the stock against his thigh. Watching the rim high above their heads, he keened his senses, seeking the glimmer of sunlight reflected off the barrel of a gun.

Three tedious hours passed uneventfully by the time the girl's brown mare trotted up a steep game trail out of the niche. Some of the tension flowed out of Will's body. The ambush he had expected never came. Single file they rode out on a broad mesa in twilight. Sagebrush cast deepening purple shadows across the flat expanse as early stars twinkled in a velvety evening sky. When the last Ranger rode to the top of the mesa, Will let out a sigh of relief. But before he turned his head to find the Lipan woman, he saw shadows moving up the trail behind Carl, and the sight sent him whirling around with the rifle to his shoulder.

"It's only them Injuns, Cap'n," Billy explained. "They've

been followin' us all along. Appears they've decided to stay with the girl.''

Will lowered the Winchester, pulling a face. The last thing they needed was a parade of half-starved Indians dogging their trail while they looked for Iron Horse. He knew now that it had been a mistake to give the hungry men mules and donkeys. Perhaps the girl would explain that following along would be dangerous. Then he reasoned that he was allowing the young woman to take the risks, guiding them to the twin mountains.

Later, riding across the dark mesa, he decided the solution was simple enough. In the morning he'd send the girl on her way back to her people. They could find the double mountains without putting anyone else's life in danger. That way his conscience would leave him alone.

Chapter
Eight

He wouldn't allow a fire, for obvious reasons. They were camped below a rocky overhang at a bend in the twisting dry wash they had followed since nightfall. Black mountains loomed around them. Will's map had identified them as the Chisos, one of the few landmarks north of Santa Elena Canyon. Dry streambeds coursed through the Chisos, like the one they navigated now. It seemed everything below Fort Davis was an endless maze of waterless streams and stark peaks. It was a forbidding place, bristling with thorns and spines everywhere. Scrub mesquites dotted lower regions where erosion left thin topsoil. Here and there the ten-foot arms of thorny ocotillo reached toward the heavens as if to beg for rainfall. At night the odd-shaped plants resembled fire-blackened skeletons against a background of dim stars. Smaller spiked yucca bristled on the slopes. Grass was scarce, or nonexistent, making travel that much harder on the horses.

Off in the distance an owl hooted softly. Seconds later a night-feeding hawk whistled overhead. Will sat beside a rock near the tethered horses, listening to the sounds from the darkness, all the while wondering if the birdcalls might also be Comanche signals. Comanches were masters of deception. Illusion won them countless battles against the white man, until the white man's number grew so large that the Indians had no places left to hide. But as Will looked around him now, he knew why Iron Horse and his followers had come to this part of Texas, for this was a place where the Comanches could make a final stand. Here they could still demonstrate their old tricks when pursuit nipped at their heels. Finding Comanches in this rugged country would be akin to seeking snowflakes in July.

A horse pawed the ground beyond the rock. Farther back in the wash where the Lipans made their camp, a burro rattled the membranes in its muzzle, making its distinctive snort. The Indians had no blankets or clothing, and when the night chill came to the mountains, they suffered from the cold. Under different circumstances he would have granted them a fire. But they were within easy striking distance of Iron Horse here, and Valdez might be prowling their back trail, seeking vengeance.

Will fingered his rifle absently, huddled inside his duster in the shadow beside the rock. Around midnight a pale quarter moon had brightened the sky, painting shadows, playing tricks on his eyes. He knew his men were worn down and needed sleep, as he too should have been after so many hard days in the saddle and restless nights spent on thin blankets, listening to Iron Horse and his renegades imitate the coyote's call. Despite his fatigue, he found he was still unable to sleep, and thus took the first night watch. Some indefinable thing was keeping him awake, nudging the darkest corners of his brain with worry.

One of the men emitted a ripping snore from the pile of blankets inside the shallow cave. The sound startled Will, increasing his heartbeat briefly, tightening his fingers around the rifle stock.

Why am I so damn jumpy tonight? he wondered. Though his eyelids were heavy, he knew sleep would not come. His weary muscles ached, and the damnable stiffness was there in his knees. The last year or two the stiffness had become more than an aggravation. There were times when his legs refused to work just right, after too many hours in a saddle and in the morning when he first got up. He'd told himself that it was a sign of old age, a warning that his days as a Texas Ranger might be numbered. When a man got too old to sit a horse from dawn till dusk, he wouldn't fit the mold Major Peoples cast for his peacekeeping force. Rangers were expected to ride from hell to breakfast without complaint. Creaking knees made any Ranger expendable, should he voice his objections to long rides. Was the time drawing near when he couldn't handle the job?

Will understood that there was more to consider than ailing joints, when the time came. For several years now it seemed the lawless men he was sworn to control were getting younger. And faster with a gun. In the business of Rangering, a man's life depended on his reflexes, and when they slowed measurably, it was time to quit, before a bullet took him down. Of late he had given plenty of thought to that kind of consequence. A younger, trigger-happy gunman might make the choice for him, if he waited too long to turn in his badge. Was it time to quit now? Before a quick-handed youngster sent him to his grave?

On the other side of things, there was the dilemma over what he would do with himself afterward, if he quit the Ranger force. He had few marketable skills: reasonably good aim with a gun, though much slower now with the passing years; some knowledge of horses and working cattle with a rope; piecemeal know-how when it came to raising a few crops, though he despised the work. What would he do if he left the Texas Rangers? Was there a market for forty-three-year-old men who retired from a lawman's job?

He'd been told that a good many Rangers retired to sheriffing positions in small towns, where the pace was slower, the risks less. Was that to be the fate of William Lee Dobbs? Keeping the peace in some out-of-the-way place from the seat of a rocking chair?

Just the thought of it made him feel sad, useless. Yet he still pondered the likelihood, thinking about his advancing age. A time would come when he had no selection, if he lived long enough with a Ranger badge pinned to his shirt. Both choices were grim: a rocking chair or an early grave. And without a wife to care for him in his old age, he'd have to face either consequence alone, a sudden death or a lonely retirement.

A movement in the Indian camp caught his eye. Someone

was walking up the wash very slowly, coming toward him. Silvery moonlight caught the dirty white cotton shirt he'd given the girl when they released her. Will puzzled over her approach, pushing off the ground so he was standing before she arrived. At six feet and two, he towered above her when she halted a few feet from the rock. In the gentle moon glow her angular face was prettier than ever, framed by hair that fell below her shoulders. She chewed her bottom lip as if in deep thought, then said, "Cold," and shivered once.

"Can't risk a fire," he said quietly, "but I've got a blanket you can use. It's gettin' late in the year, I reckon, for the nights to stay warm. I'll fetch that blanket." He strode over to the pile of saddles and removed his bedroll, shaking open his thin navy wool blanket before he offered it. She was staring at him with her arms dangling at her sides, thus he swung the blanket around her back and draped it over her shoulders. "There," he whispered. "That'll help some."

She stood before him, motionless for a time, and he wondered what was keeping her there.

"That's the best I can do," he added. Had she understood him? Was he talking too fast?

She lifted one dainty hand and slowly reached toward his face with her fingertips, until she touched his mustache lightly, feeling the bristles. He remembered that most Indians couldn't grow facial hair, perhaps explaining her curiosity. For a few seconds more she traced a finger over his mustache, then she took her hand away.

"Feels funny, I reckon," he said, not knowing what else to say just then.

"Funny?" It was a question, by her tone.

"Different, maybe. White men grow whiskers."

Her lips parted in a half smile. In the moonlight her dark eyes sparkled. "Funny," she said again, a statement now.

"Women claim it tickles when you kiss 'em," he said, certain she would have no idea what he was talking about. He'd never seen Indian men and women kiss each other, though surely they did. To make his point, he puckered and made a kissing sound. "Like this," he added, grinning.

Her face clouded. Very slowly she formed her mouth to make the same sound. When she did, Will chuckled and shook his head.

"That's it," he said. "Only you touch your lips to someone else and do it."

Her puzzlement only deepened. "Touch?" she asked, puckering once more, making the word sound harsh.

Will glanced past the girl, making sure no one was watching them, deciding to risk a demonstration. He took a step closer, lowered his face to hers, then brushed his mouth across her lips as gently as he could, making the sound. "Like that," he whispered when she did not pull away. That same warm sensation returned to his groin, reminding him that he hadn't been with a woman for quite a spell.

He fully expected her to object to what he'd done. Yet she simply stood there, watching his face expectantly, as though there might be more. Seconds later a smile crossed her mouth. "Funny," she said. "Touch."

He sighed and wagged his head. She'd gotten the words mixed up, but what did it matter? "Yeah, it feels funny when you touch my mustache," he agreed. "Now you'd better go back, before the notion gets any stronger and I do it again."

When he pointed back down the wash, she seemed to understand. Turning on her heel, she wrapped his blanket tightly around her and walked soundlessly into the darkness. He watched her depart with a touch of regret, until he remembered why they were out here in these lonesome mountains. He wasn't being paid to teach young Indian maidens how to kiss. Bringing renegade Comanches armed with repeating rifles to justice had to come first.

Dawn came clear and cool to the Chisos. Will watched the sky brighten, then turn pink. He'd slept little, dozing against the rock now and then. Whatever had been troubling him during the night was still there, undefined, a vague warning that trouble lay ahead. As the sun appeared above the mountaintops, he walked among the sleeping Rangers to awaken them with a nudge of his boot toe. He found Billy's eyes open when he came to his bedroll.

"You look like a man who's been on a three-day drunk, Cap'n," Billy observed, tossing his blanket aside, sitting up to rub his face sleepily. "How come you didn't wake me for a turn at the watch?"

Will grunted and wagged his head. "Couldn't sleep," he mumbled, glancing down the wash, to the Lipans. The Indians were already stirring, removing rope hobbles from the donkeys and mules and horses.

"What's eatin' on you, Will?" Billy asked. "We've been in a few tight spots before an' you wasn't worried. . . ."

"Can't put a finger on it," he answered, which was the truth. "Like havin' a cactus needle in your boot. It's there, but I ain't exactly sure where."

Billy climbed to his feet and stretched, yawning. "I reckon that's the reason I gave up bounty huntin'," he said. "Got where I couldn't sleep, worryin' about all the gents I'd put behind bars when they got out of jail. When a feller gets to worryin' too much about his profession, it's time he made a change. If this job's gettin' to you, Will, maybe you oughta think about doin' somethin' else for a living."

Will sighed, staring at the horizon. "I've been givin' it more thought lately," he replied. "My damn knees hurt all the time. Truth is, I wonder when I'll meet up with some owlhoot who's faster with a gun. Or the day when my reflexes are too slow an' I get a bullet in the back."

Billy nodded like he understood. "A few years back I'd earned myself a reputation with a gun," he began. A faraway look crept into his eyes. "Every green kid who had the price of a six-shooter wanted to call me out . . . I reckon to try to make a name for themselves. Most of 'em was slower'n molasses in winter, but there was a few . . ." He took a deep breath and continued. "Got to where I couldn't ride into a town without somebody knowin' my name, knowin' I was after a bounty someplace. Most folks don't look kindly on a bounty hunter. Makes it hard to find a friendly face while

you're in town. It started to eat on me . . . that, and the men
I killed. So I decided to find a different profession, if I could.

"That's the reason I signed on with the Rangers. Folks
respect this badge, and when a Ranger has to use his gun,
he's doin' it for a reason that makes some sense. This state
is plumb full of folks who can't defend themselves, Will. A
Texas Ranger is all that stands between them and some gent
with bad intentions who thinks he's good with a gun. It's
honest work.''

Will made a study of Billy's face until he finished. "I've
always felt the same way about Rangering," he said quietly.
"Somebody has to take up for gentler folks tryin' to make a
living. I never was blessed with much talent for things, but
I learned how to shoot, and most folks will tell you my word's
always been good. This job suited me, until just lately.''

Billy cracked a wry grin. "Maybe it still does, Cap'n.
Maybe you're only facing up to the truth of what we're bein'
asked to do. The major wants us to handle a job that the
whole United States Army can't get done. Maybe what's
botherin' you is that you came to the conclusion Charlie Peoples can't count, sendin' just the four of us out here like he
done. Maybe it's the major's arithmetic that's botherin' you
now.''

Will gave a dry laugh, though he was forced to consider
Billy's logic as an explanation for his uneasiness. "For a fact,
we've got our hands full this time," he agreed. "Maybe
that's why I can't get any sleep, doing all that counting inside
my head.''

Carl sat up just then, blinking sleep away as he raised the
mescal to his lips. "You shoulda let me kill that Meskin back
yonder," he said thickly. "A man don't have to see the insides of a schoolhouse very long to know that shootin' one
of the sumbitches we're after leaves less of 'em we have to
fight." He took a sip of mescal and made a face. "That's
'rithmetic any gent understands.''

Will wasn't really listening to Carl, his mind otherwise
occupied right then. The Lipan girl came toward him carrying the blanket he gave her. Her slender legs carried her

gracefully along the wash, muscles rippling in her slightly muscular thighs. Her coppery face was fixed on his, causing something to stir inside his chest, a tiny fluttering. Last night he had made up his mind to send her on her way, to keep her away from the danger posed by Iron Horse. But just now, seeing how pretty she looked in the soft morning sunlight, he decided to keep the Indians with them a while longer . . . maybe only until dark.

Carl stood up beside him, distracting him from a recollection of the kiss he'd given the girl the night before.

"Damn, she's a cute little bitch, ain't she?" Carl asked. "With all that shit washed off her, she's downright pretty."

Chapter Nine

Some sort of argument was taking place among the Lipan men when Will halted the procession around noon. The girl had ridden back to talk to them, and for a time they were engaged in animated discussion, using sign talk and clipped sounds that could barely be distinguished as words.

"Something's up back there," Billy observed, watching the Indians from the back of his horse. "That older Injun keeps using the sign for Comanches. Figures he's afraid to go any farther, on account of bein' close to Iron Horse. Might as well tell 'em they can ride off, Cap'n. They won't be any help if we strike those renegades. Some are liable to get killed when the shootin' starts."

"I'd been figurin' a way to tell the girl," Will remarked. "She don't speak much English, but she oughta understand when I tell her to head back home. We can find that pair of mountains ourselves, now that we're headed the right direction."

Leon edged his horse up to Will's, leading the string of spare mounts. "I've got that feelin' again, Cap'n," he said, scanning the slopes around them. "Somebody's watchin' us. Had the feelin' all morning."

"You're a superstitious son of a bitch," Carl spat, grimacing. "There ain't nothin' out there 'cept lizards an' snakes, Leon. That damn feelin' ain't nothin' but tight longjohns squeezin' your balls. If you had a lick of sense, you'd know that. Squeezed balls make a man nervous."

"Somebody's out there," Leon insisted, staring off. "If you wasn't drunk on that mescal, you'd know it too."

"I ain't drunk," Carl said, admiring what was left in the bottle when he pulled it from a pocket of his duster. "I ain't sick, either, on account of I've got my medicine. You keep on worryin' like that, partner, and you'll wind up in one of them asylums for crazy folks."

Will was watching the girl. She kept pointing northwest, saying something to the men gathered around her mare. The scrawny Indians were a pitiful lot, and Will knew Billy was right about sending them away before they encountered Iron Horse.

"We'll need water for these horses mighty soon," Billy remarked, ending Will's attention to the Lipans. "That's liable to be a man-sized job, findin' any water in these mountains."

"Maybe the girl knows where there's a spring," Will offered absently, examining their surroundings for a stand of trees, anything that might indicate water. His dun was gaunt-flanked, as were the rest of the animals, sweating profusely in the midday heat with the burden of a rider. "Wish the hell it would rain," he added, tilting his face skyward briefly, finding no clouds, only a merciless West Texas sun. A dry wind came at them from the west, smelling of dust, holding no promise of rain.

The girl swung her mare and struck a trot back toward the Rangers. Though it was often hard to read any change in her expression, tiny crow's-feet now webbed beside her eyes, and her brow was pinched, as if she were scowling. She halted the mare in front of Will and pointed back to the men. "No go," she said, shaking her head back and forth. "Afraid Iron Horse."

"I understand," Will answered. "All of you must leave. Go back to your village. We'll find Iron Horse on our own."

She pointed to herself. "I go."

Will inclined his head and said "No," gently. "We go alone." Then he remembered the horses. "Can you show us where to find water?"

The girl turned her gaze north, indicating a direction with

her hand. "Water," she said, forming the word slowly, then she made a sign for drinking with a cupped palm.

"Show us," Will said. "Our horses have to have water before we can look for Iron Horse." He lifted his reins and turned the dun in the right direction.

The mare started forward at a walk. Will fell in behind and heard the other horses move off. The girl was taking them toward a distant stretch of low foothills at the base of a craggy black peak to the north. In the heat haze boiling up from the sunbaked hills, Will thought he could make out a spot where a strip of faint green colored the land. It could be a stand of trees several miles away, had the dancing heat waves not prevented him from seeing clearly. Many a thirsty man had died in wasteland such as this, trusting the watery illusions beckoning from a desert floor.

For a time he listened to the clatter of horseshoes, his mind a blank, senses dulled by lack of sleep. Soon the monotony of the landscape put him dozing off in the saddle. Following the girl required no watchfulness on his part. Slumped aboard the dun, he drifted into foggy daydreams, awakening now and then with a jolt when he tilted out of the saddle. Sweat had begun to pour down from his hat brim, and his shirt clung wetly to his skin inside the duster. He dreamed vague dreams about water when he noticed that his tongue felt like it was coated with sand.

He wondered if he might still be dreaming when he awoke to find a pool of sparkling water before him. His horse had its muzzle buried in the depths of a tiny spring pocketed by huge boulders. Will blinked and shook his head to clear it of sleep fog.

Billy sat his horse beside Will. "You was dozin', Cap'n," he said. "A time or two I figured you was gonna fall off on your head. It'll be dark soon. We can camp here for the night."

Will looked around him, to get his bearings. They had ridden to the base of the black mountain and he must have slept through most of the ride. Carl and Leon watered their horses on the far side of the pool, but when he gazed around, he couldn't find the Lipan girl or the rest of the Indians.

"Where'd the others go?" he asked sleepily.

Billy shrugged, aiming a thumb over his shoulder. "They took off back yonder a ways, most of 'em. That girl and one of them older Injuns stayed with us. They rode up the side of that mountain to have a look around, I suppose."

Will merely grunted, examining the rock-strewn low spot where they found the spring. There was plenty of dry bunch grass for the horses among the rocks, enough to fill their bellies before daybreak. "Makin' camp here sounds good," he said. It required a great deal of effort when he lifted a boot from the stirrup and swung it over the dun's rump to dismount. When his feet touched the ground, a stab of pain awakened in his knees. For a moment he stood beside his horse holding on to the saddle horn, working the stiffness from his aching legs.

He looked down their back trail when his legs would work, walking slowly away from the thirsty horses for a view of the land across which they had come. Satisfied that the hills were empty, he aimed a look up the mountain above the spring.

High on a switchback he glimpsed the rumps of two horses poorly hidden by a stand of brush. Looking closely, he found the woman near the edge of the thicket, shading her eyes from a late-day sun with the palm of her hand. For a short while he watched her, until the horses around the spring started to drift away to graze. Idly he wondered what the girl was looking at up there, staying longer than he figured was necessary if there was nothing to see.

Later he heard two horses coming down the face of the mountain at a trot, and puzzled over the apparent haste. He looked toward the girl when both horses reached the bottom of the slope.

She kicked her mare to a gallop, sending warning signals to Will's sleepy brain. Running horses usually spelled trouble in his experience.

The girl and the older Indian brought their horses to a halt in front of him. Before the dust around them settled, the girl was pointing to the west.

"Sata Teichas," she cried with urgency, as though he would know what she meant.

And he did understand her, for the name Sata Teichas brought back unwanted memories, old fears. It was the name Comanches called themselves, meaning "the People" in the Comanche tongue. He wheeled toward the western horizon and narrowed his eyes to keep out the brilliance of a setting sun.

For several silent minutes all four Rangers studied the distant slopes and canyons, until Will concluded there was nothing to see. He turned to the girl. "How many?" he asked in a cottony voice, his mouth gone dry.

She raised just one finger and held it aloft. Then she said, "Iron Horse," very softly, slowly, her dark eyes wider than before.

Will gave the landscape yet another examination, halting his gaze when he came to a formation of rock, or a clump of brush. The sun cast long shadows now, making it harder to find a shape among the rocks and plants that might belong to a man.

"I told you somebody was out there," Leon said, standing at the front of the spare mounts. His rifle was slung loosely in one hand, balanced. "We'd better post an extra guard tonight," he added. "They'd like nothin' better than to put us afoot way out here."

"Let 'em come," Carl growled, facing the sunset, his eyes moving swiftly from one spot to the next. A meaty hand fisted around the stock of the shotgun slung below his shoulder. "I'm damn tired of wanderin' all over this godforsaken place anyways. It'd suit the hell outta me if we got this over with."

"Maybe he's just looking us over," Will said quietly. "Taking a count, to see how many he's up against. From here on out we ride real careful. It's a Comanche's nature to set a trap for his enemies, maybe try to lure us into following him into an ambush someplace."

Billy had been silent until now. He removed his hat and sleeved sweat from his forehead. "Could be that's why he showed himself just now, Cap'n. Hopin' we'd see him and ride that direction come daylight. Occurs to me we could try to fool him after it gets dark. Build a big fire right here, so he could see it. Then ride north real careful and slow, circle around behind him. If we kept these horses real quiet ridin' this rock, we stand a chance of gettin' behind him before the sun comes up. Worst of it is, we don't know how many warriors he's got with him. If it's a big bunch, we might get ourselves in a fix."

Will thought about Billy's plan, and the risks. "We've got to face those odds sooner or later," he said. "It might work, slippin' around behind him. That way, we'd have the element of surprise on our side. We could pick the spot where we fought him."

"Suits the hell outta me," Carl said impatiently. "Sooner we start fightin' Injuns, the quicker we'll get back to San Antone."

Will glanced to Leon, awaiting his opinion. Leon's eyelids batted while he stared at the land below the setting sun.

"It's okay by me, Cap'n," Leon said. "Makes just as much sense as sittin' here all night. Only thing is, we're takin' a chance of runnin' into 'em in the dark while we're movin' around. Won't be much moon. . . ."

"Hell, that ain't no problem," Carl argued. "I always could see like a barn owl at night . . . learned it stealin' watermelons from old man Sikes's orchard when I was a kid. I'll keep my eyes peeled tonight, if that's all that's worryin' you."

Will scoured the western valleys and slopes until his eyes hurt from the sun's slanted rays. Had the girl really seen Iron Horse out there? She had seemed sure of the Indian's identity. Had she been a prisoner in one of the cages when Iron Horse came to the Comanchero camp to trade for rifles? Had Iron Horse been the one who captured her?

He decided to ask her a few questions. When he swung

away from the sunset, she was watching his face. "Are you sure it was Iron Horse?" he asked.

She nodded and made the sign of the snake. The Lipan warrior sitting his horse beside her also made the sign, then he pointed west.

Will knew there was no other conclusion left. Both Indians were sure of what they had seen. Then it occurred to him that if the girl could recognize the renegade chieftain, she would also know how many men rode with him. "How many warriors are with Iron Horse?" he asked.

The girl didn't answer him. Instead, she said something to the other Lipan, and received an answer sounding like a series of grunts. The warrior let go of his reins and lifted ten fingers. Then the woman looked at Will again, leaving the impression that she couldn't say what the ten fingers indicated.

"Ten men," Will said softly. "It coulda been worse."

"This ain't gonna be much of a fight, Cap'n," he heard Carl say. "We already whipped fourteen Meskins back there at Gold Tooth's hideout. Killin' ten Injuns won't take no time at all, if the yellow bastards will show themselves."

Carl's response had been predictable enough. But down deep, Will knew Carl didn't understand the nature of the savages they were up against. "That's a part of the problem, Carl," Will said tiredly, with a shrug. "A Comanche's too smart to come at an enemy from the front. It's the reason Iron Horse an' his bunch are still on the loose out here, 'stead of on a reservation. He's too smart to let us corner him . . . too wily to ride out in plain sight. This is gonna be like tryin' to grab a fistful of smoke. You'll think you've got him boxed in, only he won't be there." Will took a deep breath, remembering other times he fought the elusive Comanches. "We can try Billy's plan, but it ain't likely to work. Best thing we can do is find his stronghold . . . burn him out, all his food and ammunition and their winter lodges. But you can count on him puttin' up one hell of a fight before he allows that to happen. He'll know they can't survive the winter without food, or a place to hide when the snows come."

"You reckon it snows in this part of Texas?" Leon asked,

with a look at the sky. "Can't hardly imagine such a thing, hot as it gets out here."

Will started back toward the horses. "I spent some time in El Paso a few years back," he remembered. "Coldest damn place I'd ever been . . . sleet and snow all over the ground that winter. Ain't nothin' between here and the Dakotas 'cept a few mountains. If we're still here when the first blue norther hits, you'll understand what I mean about the cold."

He trudged over to the spring and loosened the dun's cinch so the horse could graze freely, wondering if he and his men would still be wandering these same mountains in December, chasing Comanche shadows. He knew he couldn't explain what it was like to fight a race of men who could simply vanish into thin air.

Chapter Ten

Horses walking. Until now he'd always thought of it as a soft sound, the muted clop of a hoof when it struck the ground, or the occasional harsh click of a horseshoe moving across a pebble here and there. But tonight, attempting to skirt a suspected Comanche position somewhere to the south, the sounds of their horses walking could only be likened to the rattle of gunfire. Will was sure Iron Horse could hear the horses, even from miles away.

It's my nerves, he thought. He'd spent too much time thinking about that missing plug of Horace Biggs's hair, the flinty gleam of bone atop his skull that next morning, when they found him. And that terrible moment of cowardice when he hid behind a stone wall with his hands trembling, gripping a rifle he was afraid to use. There had been similar moments, those years he rode with Hood, but always, in the back of his mind, there had been a way to escape. Riding a slow circle around a bunch of renegade Comanches in the dark brought back some of that same gnawing fear he'd felt then.

The girl and the Lipan warrior rode in front of Leon at the back of the procession, for Will had deemed it too dangerous after sighting Iron Horse to send them in another direction. Will cursed himself silently now, for allowing the woman to stay. Should Iron Horse waylay them tonight with repeating rifles, it could easily cost the girl her life. She didn't owe the Rangers anything in the first place, certainly not enough to put her life on the line to guide them toward the renegade stronghold. Will knew he shouldn't have permitted it. A moment of weakness, perhaps simple desire for a beautiful girl, altered his better judgment.

At the crest of a rise between two slopes, Billy halted his bay abruptly and stood in his stirrups, gazing south. Carl sat beside him, holding his roan in check, looking in the same direction. For a pair of anxious hours they had ridden through the dark, guided only by faint starlight. Will's nerves were like fiddle strings, waiting for Billy to identify whatever was holding his attention for so long.

When Will's impatience grew stronger, he heeled the dun forward and rode up to Billy. "What is it?" he whispered hoarsely. The mountains and hills to the south seemed empty, still as death itself.

"This horse sensed somethin' out there," Billy replied. "Cocked its head this way and flared its nostrils. Might have smelled somethin' on the wind, Cap'n. A horse has got a keen sense of smell when it's range-bred, like this bay."

A warm southwesterly night wind swept across the rise, but to Will the wind carried no scent. "Smells like dust," he said, "but it pays to be careful."

They sat motionless for several minutes more, listening to the silence around them. Now and then one of their horses stamped a hoof or rattled a curb chain, but there were no sounds from the south, nor movement among the night shadows below the rise.

"Can't see a thing," Carl said later. A gust of wind ruffled the tails of his duster about his feet, flapping cloth against a spur rowel, making a musical tinkle. Carl's beard-stubbled cheeks were drawn tight across his face. His bushy eyebrows knitted, then relaxed.

Billy's bay snorted suddenly and bowed its neck.

"Easy, hoss," Billy whispered, patting the gelding's mane gently. "There's somethin' out there, Cap'n. This bay can smell it, an' it don't like the way it smells."

"Maybe it's just a polecat," Carl said. "Can't say as I like the way they smell, either."

Billy shook his head from side to side. "A horse recognizes a skunk smell. No reason to be afraid of it. Whatever's out there, my bay acts scared of it. Could be an Injun . . . maybe more'n just one.''

"Let's get off the top of this ridge," Will said quickly. "We make good targets, sittin' up here. Head for those rocks, Billy, but do it slow an' careful-like."

Billy swung his horse southwest when he heard Will's order and started for a rocky knob below the crest of the rise. The others followed Billy in an uneven line, holding their horses to a walk. The animals' hooves made more noise than Will wanted to hear right then, but more than anything else, he sought the safety of the knob. Until they knew what alerted Billy's horse, Will was determined to find some cover and wait things out.

They crossed the distance to the base of the rock hill at a snail's pace, jangling Will's nerves that much more. Only when Leon led the last spare mount behind the hill did Will allow himself to relax a little. He took a moment to examine their surroundings, the deep shadows at the base of the outcrop, before stepping to the ground with his Winchester. His right boot had no more than touched the earth when a shot rang out.

Their horses bolted as the explosion echoed from the hills below the knob. Will held tightly to the dun's reins while churning hooves clattered around him, ruining his chance to guess the direction of the shot. Until the horses settled, men and animals swirled before him, inky shadows in the night.

He heard Carl mutter a curse, then his boots were scrambling up the rock face to the top of the knob. A rifle barrel gleamed in his hands. When his bulky outline was visible behind the crest of the jagged rocks, the noises stopped. "Can't see a damn thing," he growled softly, his head turning this way and that.

"I saw the muzzle flash," Leon whispered among the shadowy shapes of the horses. "Hold these broncs, Billy. I'll send a dose of lead down there."

Billy hurried over to grab the lead ropes and reins. The lone gunshot puzzled Will. Why were there no more? He crouched and took a look behind them, along the crest of the ridge where they had been moments before. Was the shot merely intended to distract them while the Comanches slipped around to the rear?

Leon's spurs jingled away to the west. He trotted off from the protection of the knob brazenly, as though he meant to draw the Indians' fire by showing himself. A shallow ravine lay to the west of the outcrop, and Leon made for it in a running crouch, dodging back and forth until he dropped out of sight into the mouth of the ravine.

Will's heart was racing now. They had almost ridden head-long into a trap, blinded by the dark. Iron Horse had guessed the Rangers' plan all too easily. The campfire they left burning back at the spring had not fooled him at all.

Their back trail was clear, although he cautioned himself not to trust his eyes when their adversaries were Comanches. Thus he scanned the ridge again, more carefully this time, lingering when he saw a darker shadow until he was sure an Indian wasn't hiding in it. A silence surrounded the knob, now that the horses had calmed. But Will did not trust the silence either, any more than he trusted the emptiness he saw.

Sudden gunfire erupted from the west, from the draw where Leon had disappeared. Four, five, then a sixth explosion rocked the stillness. Then a faint cry sounded far below the knob.

"He got the son of a bitch!" Carl hissed from the top of the rock. "Ol' Leon's got all the luck."

Will took his eyes off the ridge reluctantly, when he heard the distant cry of pain. Straightening up from a battle-ready crouch, he missed the glint of gun metal at the top of the rise behind him.

The roar of a rifle sent him sprawling on his face beneath the whine of a speeding slug. A ball of molten lead whacked dully into the shoulder of one of the spare horses near Billy. The animal reared and whickered in terror, pawing its fore-feet, jerking the lead rope from Billy's hand. The gelding bawled and fell over on its side, thumping heavily against the ground, its hooves thrashing. The rest of the horses shied, fighting the restraint of reins and ropes, as Will rolled to one side and aimed his Winchester at the ridge.

He fired off a hasty shot without a target, hoping only to keep the Comanche pinned down. When the rifle kicked against Will's shoulder, the sound deafened him to the sounds of milling horses. He levered the empty shell casing from the firing chamber as quickly as he could, hoping that Billy and Carl could somehow manage to hang on to the horses before the Comanche sniper killed them one at a time, leaving the Rangers afoot. Above all else, they must save the horses.

A shot boomed from the black spines of a yucca plant high on the ridge, a spit of yellow fire flickering briefly amid the blast. A bullet sizzled above Will and ricocheted off the rock somewhere behind him, singing harmlessly way. Will sighted in on the muzzle flash and squeezed the trigger. The rifle slammed into him, cracking like a clap of thunder. A stab of flame left the muzzle, and he thought he saw the yucca spines quiver atop the ridge. He levered and fired again mechanically. This time he was sure the plant moved as gun smoke wafted away from his rifle—the yucca was gone.

A gun pounded behind Will, two shots in rapid succession from the top of the knob. "Dirty sumbitches are hard to see," Carl grumbled, working the firing mechanism on his Winchester. Empty shell jackets tumbled hollowly down the rock. A horse snorted somewhere in the darkness, then all was quiet. Will's eyes moved slowly up and down the starlit ridge. Nothing moved.

Despite the night chill, sweat trickled down Will's checks, salty when he licked his lips. His heart was hammering inside his shirt above the dull ringing in his ears. He suspected that the Indians were moving around them now, seeking better firing positions. The knob would only protect the Rangers if they could keep it between them and the enemy. Will let out a rasping breath. Iron Horse would know this and he would keep circling, firing into the Rangers' exposed flanks until all the horses had been killed. Then he could wait for daybreak and cut the Rangers down one at a time, with a circle of marksmen around the knob.

Muffled gunfire erupted from the ravine, bringing Will to a crouch suddenly. Four shots rattled, then the silence returned as quickly as it ended. Had Leon surprised one of the Comanches as they tried to circle them? There was, however, a darker possibility. The Comanches might have surprised Leon and cut him down. The Indians had Winchesters, thus there was no way to distinguish between the sounds.

"You didn't send enough men this time, Charlie," Will whispered to himself. His hands were damp around the rifle stock, awaiting the Comanches' next move. The ridge behind them was clear, for now. But if Iron Horse possessed the cunning his people were known for, he would send someone back to the ridge and the shooting would start again.

The wounded horse struggled to regain its feet, groaning pitifully when its feeble efforts failed. Will risked a look over his shoulder and found the girl and the Lipan warrior huddled beside the riderless horses at the base of the knob. It was some consolation to learn they were still alive, though Will wondered just how long the condition would last. He thought about Leon then. Had the foolhardy Ranger charged recklessly into the brunt of the Comanche attack?

"Can't see a goddamn thing out there," Carl complained. "If those yellow sumbitches had any backbone, they'd show themselves."

It was little satisfaction that Carl was learning what fighting Comanches was like. A Comanche only allowed himself to be seen when he had a purpose behind it. "Can you see Leon out there?" he asked, his worries deepening.

"If I could, he'd probably be dead," Carl answered. "Ol' Leon can take care of himself, Cap'n. Don't fret over that fool's whereabouts. I'll bet he's out there someplace killin' Comanches. He always did have all the luck."

Will tried to find Billy in the darkness. A shadow in a flat-brim hat stood near the saddled horses, peering over the neck of one gelding. "See anything, Billy?" Will asked quietly.

"Nary a thing," Billy replied, "but I'm gettin' a touch

worried 'bout Leon, Cap'n. If you'll hang on to these broncs fer a spell, I'll head over to that draw an' see if'n I can find him. He's out there all by his lonesome an' he's liable to need a hand.''

"He shouldn't have gone off by himself like that," Will remarked. He straightened up cautiously and examined the ridge again. Backing toward the horses, he pondered the wisdom of allowing Billy to go looking for the missing Ranger. Iron Horse would be looking for the chance to split the forces of his enemies.

"I wouldn't go lookin' for him if I was you," Carl offered from his perch atop the knob. "He's liable to shoot anything that moves right about now. When he gets on a killin' spree, he ain't got good sense. He ain't all that smart in the first place, if the truth was told."

Will sighed. "We'll give him a few minutes," he said, entering the group of horses. He caught a glimpse of the girl's face. Her eyes were round with terror. "Stay down," he told her, then he crept over to Billy and stood for a time, watching their dark surroundings. "Maybe they pulled back," he said later, though he doubted such wishful thinking. Iron Horse wouldn't give up so easily, knowing he had the advantage now.

A tinkling sound came from the draw. It sent Will whirling around with his Winchester leveled.

"That was a spur," Billy whispered. "Hold your fire."

A shadow moved in the dark bowels of the ravine. Someone was walking slowly along the bottom of the draw. A moment later Will recognized the outline of Leon's hat in the darkness. "That's Leon," he said softly. "He's pullin' something behind him. . . ."

Spurs clanked out of the mouth of the ravine. Leon carried his Winchester over his shoulder, dragging some dark object behind him Will couldn't identify. Whatever it was, Leon apparently prized it enough to risk walking boldly across open ground to drag it toward the knob.

"It's an Injun," Carl said. "He's got a fistful of that Injun's hair. He's gone plumb out of his mind this time. . . ."

Now Will could see the Comanche's feet bouncing life-lessly over the hardpan. Leaning into the weight of the pull, Leon trudged up the gradual slope toward the Rangers, spurs banging like the rhythmic beat of a drum.

"It's me, Cap'n," Leon advised needlessly. "Those Co-manches cleared out a while ago. I got this one, but the rest of 'em got away clean. Thought I nicked one more, a big feller, but he just shook his fist at me whilst I was loadin' my gun an' then he was gone." Leon was out of breath by the time he reached the horses. "You was right about one thing, Cap'n," he gasped, hauling the dead Comanche to one of the spare horses, where he promptly dropped his head on the ground, making a wet sound. "These sumbitches are hard to shoot. I had one dead in my sights, but he weren't where he was supposed to be when my bullet got there."

Will walked over to Leon. "Why'd you drag that dead Indian up here?" he asked.

Leon shrugged and spread his ropelike arms to explain. "Just wanted to show Carl an' Billy what he looked like, Cap'n. None of the rest of us ever saw a Comanche afore this." He looked up at Carl. "Come down an' have a look, partner," he said, grinning in the faint light from above. "They's bigger'n a Lipan. Taller by a foot or more. But they die just as quick as anybody else. Come look at this hole I blowed in his head."

Will swung away from Leon, irritated by his casual dis-cussion of death. The wounded horse was floundering again. Someone needed to put it out of its misery.

Chapter
Eleven

Brittle brush mottled the valley floor with irregular patches of shade. Hackberry bushes grew in thick clusters higher on the slopes, providing dense thickets where a man could hide. Along the rim of the valley, scrub pine trees bearing meager tufts of needles at the ends of barren branches swayed gently on breaths of cool air washing down from the Christmas peaks. Mexican vaqueros called the small pines "pinion," Will remembered. Lying flat on a rock ledge high above the valley, his eyes followed a dim game trail across the brushy flat below, the route they must follow to reach the pair of dark mountains looming to the northwest. The twin peaks were still a day's ride for the Rangers, a day of dangerous travel if Santiago Cortez and the Lipan girl were right about what awaited them in those stark slabs of rock. Somewhere in the crags and hollows was a hiding place, a natural fortress where Iron Horse felt safe. Will meant to find the renegades' secret stronghold, to destroy the Comanches' reserves of food and ammunition. He knew the price of making such a bold move would come high. Iron Horse would fight with all his cunning to protect his sanctuary. It promised to be a deadly confrontation, if Will could only lead his men to the right spot. Miles of risky travel had to be negotiated first, like the valley yawning below the ledge. Iron Horse wouldn't wait until the Rangers got close. He would set traps for them along the way, hoping to thin the number of his enemies before they found his winter lodges.

"We'll be sittin' ducks down there," Billy remarked. He lay beside Will, examining the trail across the valley.

Since dawn they had ridden cautiously westward, after spending uneasy hours before sunrise at the base of the knob where Iron Horse tried to ambush them. As impossible as it seemed, the land turned even more forbidding as they rode through the morning hours. They had begun a steady climb shortly after daybreak, following rock-strewn ravines higher into the Christmas range, often forced to ride up long switchbacks in plain sight, the only footing their horses could manage when steep-walled ravines ended. They arrived at this deep valley when the sun was directly overhead. But when Will saw what awaited them if they crossed the valley in broad daylight, he ordered a halt to consider their chances.

"Too many places where they could bushwhack us," Will said, studying a hackberry thicket close to the game trail. "No way to make sure that brush down there isn't hiding a sharpshooter. We'd be fools to ride it. We'll have to find a way around."

Sheer mountain slopes surrounded the valley on all sides. Will scanned the rock faces for a ledge where they might lead their horses around. Massive walls of lichen-covered stone jutted into the sky everywhere he looked. A mountain goat would have trouble navigating either side of the valley rim.

"Can't see no way to skirt it," Billy observed, sweeping the walls north and south. He looked down at the valley floor again, frowning. "Not much choice, Cap'n," he said. "We backtrack, or fight our way across that valley."

Will pulled back from the ledge and stood up. Carl and Leon were waiting with the Lipans at a rock pile where the deer trail bent sharply to begin a steep descent into the valley. Will had known the ride down would be too dangerous without making sure of things below. Now he was certain the ride down would have been a poor choice.

"What's the holdup, Cap'n?" Carl asked when Will and Billy returned to the horses. Carl was chewing on a pinion nut. The ground below the stunted pines was littered with dried nut husks.

"We're liable to get shot full o' holes if we go any farther,'' Will replied, a gust of chilly wind outlining his angular frame inside his duster. Carl's impatience with their slow pace had been evident all morning. His grumbling and complaining had begun to rankle Will. Carl had finished the last of his mescal just before dawn, bringing the unwanted change in his mood shortly thereafter. "I figure it'll add a couple of extra days for us to ride around," Will added. "But the way I see it, we've got no choice."

Carl's face darkened. "I'll go down there first an' clear the way," he said. "You boys can wait here till I say it's okay to come down. Those Injuns are scared of a fight, Cap'n," he continued, tossing a fistful of pinion nuts aside.

As Will was about to speak, he heard the girl say something to her Lipan companion. The old man was wrapped in Billy's blanket to keep out the cold wind, and when the girl spoke to him, he snaked a bony arm from a fold in the bed cover, pointing to the top of a mountain on the north side of the valley. His reply made no sense, but Will knew he was telling the girl about a way around.

"Come," the woman said, beckoning to Will. She wheeled her mare and started back down the game trail in the direction they had come, with the Lipan close at her heels.

"Let's see where they take us," Will said, climbing into his saddle.

"Hope it ain't very damn far," Carl muttered, swinging heavily aboard his roan. "I'm startin' to get itchy all over, like I come down with a case of the hives."

Leon made a sour face just as Will trotted his dun past the two men. "You're just soberin' up, partner," Leon said. "That's all it is. If you hadn't been drunk last night, you coulda killed a few of them sneaky red bastards. When a man's too drunk to see straight, he can't hardly expect straight shootin'."

"Wasn't no such thing," Carl grumbled, reining his horse after Will's. "Mescal tastes like shit. Couldn't hardly drink it. Had to force myself."

Leon's dry laugh cackled above the rattle of horseshoes as they rode east, away from the valley.

They walked along a windswept ledge, leading their horses. A look down was enough to churn Will's stomach, so he avoided it and kept his eyes on the Lipan shrouded in his blue blanket, leading the way. The narrow ledge was barely wide enough for a horse. Below, a drop of a thousand feet awaited the man or animal making a careless placement of a foot. The Lipan had seemed sure that everyone could make the treacherous footing safely; he kept shaking his head, waving for the others to follow him. There were faint deer tracks in places along the ledge, though Will understood that they were simply proof of a deer's successful travels here. Men and horses might not enjoy the same success. He tried not to think about it, what it would be like to feel a boot give way, to feel himself falling toward the rocks below.

Gusts of wind howled around them. A bank of dark clouds had begun to build to the north, and the wind had turned colder. At these higher elevations they could expect most any kind of weather late in the fall. Even snow. Will forced his concentration on the placement of each foot, pushing thoughts about the weather from his mind.

A nerve-wracking hour of twists and turns passed, crossing the far side of the peaks north of the valley. At infrequent wide spots in the ledge, Will turned around to check on his men. Carl's face was a mask of determined concentration while he walked the slim rock ledge. Billy's hat brim prevented Will from seeing the Ranger's face, bent down like it was toward his footing. Leon seemed unconcerned by the heights, ambling along at the rear without expression. "He's too crazy to be scared of falling," Will whispered, starting off again behind the Lipan and the girl.

Half an hour later he allowed himself a brief moment of celebration when the ledge widened onto a tree-studded slope. The way down would be easier, and they could ride it. The Lipan led his horse to one side and mounted, tucking the blanket around his legs and chest. He gave Will a half smile, pointing to a gentler drop off the side of the mountain, worn smooth by deer tracks.

"It's gonna rain," Billy said behind Will, mounting his horse, "I'm damn glad we didn't have to make that walk when it was slippery."

Carl's expression was decidedly unhappy when he stuck a boot into his stirrup. "I could goddamn sure use a drink," he said with a grunt when he hauled his weight over the saddle. "A man with the shakes has got no business travelin' a place like that. I'd have given a month's pay fer a jug back yonder, even a jug of that shitty-tastin' mescal."

"You ain't got no taste in the first place," Leon said, grinning, urging his horse past Carl, pulling the three remaining spare mounts behind him. He rode up to Will. "Some of us oughta change saddles to this fresh stock," he said. "We've put some hard miles on our broncs an' they could use a rest."

Will nodded, aiming a look down the mountain slope. "When we get to those trees, you and Carl and Billy can saddle the spares. This dun's thankful he didn't fall off that ledge, so he won't object to carryin a load awhile longer. While we're changin' saddles, we can pass around some of that jerky. Real suddenlike, my belly got settled down, and now it's tellin' me I'm hungry."

He turned the dun down the trail and settled against the back of his saddle, feeling better about things. Crossing the ledge had given them a chance to ride around a likely Comanche ambush. Once again they were indebted to the Lipans, first for the spring, and now for guiding them around the valley. Freeing the Comancheros' Lipan prisoners had been a simple act of kindness, but it was paying off handsomely in the search for Iron Horse. And as an aside, the girl provided some mighty pretty scenery, when she wasn't covered up inside his blanket like she was now.

The dun struck a trot to reach the front of the procession, then Will slowed it with a bump on the curb chain. Beginning the descent, he cast a look at the dark clouds stretching across the horizon, and as he scented the northerly wind, he was sure he smelled rain.

At the bottom of the slope he rode into a stand of taller pinion pines and halted his gelding. Swinging down to wait for the others, he took a look at the faint scar in the rocks high above them, where they'd made the dangerous passage along the mountaintops. Then he shook his head, thankful to be alive, and carried a bundle of jerky to give to the men and the girl.

Dry pine needles crunched softly beneath his boots while he handed out strips of meat. He came to the girl last and gave her some of the jerky, dimly aware of the smell of pine around them, or that dark clouds scudded across the sky overhead, blotting out the sun.

"We're grateful to your friend for showing us the way," he said gently, with a smile.

She bit off a mouthful of meat and chewed silently, avoiding his stare.

"Tell me your name," he asked. "All this time, and I haven't known what to call you. . . ."

"Osate," she said, pointing to herself. "I called Osate," then she pointed to a bird on a nearby pine limb. "Osate," she said again.

"It's a pretty name," he said quietly, so the others wouldn't hear him. "I am called Will."

Her eyes clouded with doubt. "Called Cap-en," she replied, having difficulty with the last word.

He laughed. "They call me Captain," he said. "It's my rank with the Texas Rangers, not my name."

She did not understand—he saw it in her face. "You can call me Cap'n, if you like," he added. "I don't reckon it matters much, since I can't explain it." He pointed to the Lipan warrior. "What is he called?" Will asked.

"Tasa," she answered quickly, filling her cheeks with meat again.

The saddle changes were finished before Will could ask the girl about the location of her people's village. If he could manage it, he wanted to send Osate and Tasa away, before they came any closer to a fight with Iron Horse. The two gentle Lipans had done enough to assist them, and now it was time to get them out of harm's way, before the deadly battle began in earnest.

"We're ready to ride, Cap'n," Carl said, mounting a short-coupled black gelding, the only horse among the spares with enough muscle to carry Carl's weight. The black pranced nervously, sidestepping, until it felt a pull on the bit in its mouth. Carl scowled down at the black's ears. "This bastard needs a drink worse'n me," he added gruffly, which evoked a chuckle from Leon and a grin from Billy.

Will turned away from Osate, deciding to wait for a better time to start the Lipans on their way back home. It was only a guess, but he figured the Indians had been captured somewhere farther west, in what was called New Mexico Territory. The newspaper in San Antone published a story sometime back, that a few Apache bands and some smaller tribes had been pushed westward by army patrols to the dry deserts and mountain ranges of the territory. Peaceful Lipans would not occupy traditional Comanche hunting ground, fearing reprisal. The Lipan prisoners they found with Gold Tooth Valdez had likely been captured many miles to the west, probably by Iron Horse and his band, as barter for repeating rifles. Sending a young girl and her defenseless companion across distances like that was a decision Will wasn't quite ready to make. After all, he owed the pair of Indians something for what they'd done to help the Rangers.

He mounted the dun, glancing sideways when Osate swung over the mare's back. There was something about the slender girl that caught his attention too often, making him feel foolish when he thought about it. Hell, she was an Indian, and the last time he looked in a mirror, he was still a white man.

Chapter Twelve

Sheets of rain came horizontally on mighty gusts of wind. The first few drops pattering down on Will's hat were the size of bird's eggs, making a popping noise when they fell on the brim. Will raised the collar on his duster and hunkered down inside it. Soon a rivulet of water fell in front of his eyes where the hat brim drooped to keep the sun off his face. Thunder rumbled in the dark skies overhead. Occasional bolts of lightning snapped from the clouds, brightening the shapes of the twin mountains before them. Sodden hoofbeats were lost in the claps of thunder and the rattle of pelting raindrops on wet canvas coats. The storm raged, and if anything, seemed to be worsening.

Will halted his horse in the protection of some pines, to look back at the rain-soaked riders behind him. Osate and Tasa were hooded silhouettes on the backs of their horses, their faces hidden in the folds of blankets. Carl was little more than a bulky outline, a hat and a water-drenched coat atop a plodding black horse. Will waited in the trees until he saw Leon at the rear, leading the rest of the horses through puddles of rainwater. Billy had ridden too far out in front; Will lost sight of him, but wanted to make sure the others were together before he rode off in search of Billy.

It would be dark soon. The painfully slow walk along the high mountain ledge had used up most of the daylight. The storm would add too much to the risks of riding at night. Will meant to find a campsite where they could wait out the howling winds and rain. It promised to be a miserable night, trying to sleep in wet blankets, if they slept at all. He'd sent

Billy ahead to seek the driest spot he could find, if such a thing existed in a downpour. In the blinding rain, Billy had lengthened the distance and ridden out of sight a few minutes earlier, and the torrent falling from the sky had washed out his scant tracks. Will understood the danger. If they allowed themselves to be separated by the storm, a man riding alone made an easy victim for Iron Horse's sharpshooters. A battle-seasoned veteran would know how to use the cover of the storm to best advantage, and it was a sure bet Iron Horse had plenty of battle experience. No amount of hardship prevented a Comanche from making war. They seemed to thrive on adversity. The storm would be an invitation to attack, one a crafty war leader like Iron Horse couldn't ignore.

"Wait here," Will shouted when Carl rode up beside him. "Billy rode off someplace, looking for a dry spot. I'll try to find him. Keep the others right here, and keep your eyes open. Those Comanches are liable to use this rain for cover. Stay in these trees, an' wait till I get back."

Carl nodded, spilling water from his hat brim when he moved his head. A clap of thunder drowned out his reply.

Will reined the dun out of the trees, squinting to see any movement in the curtain of rainfall before he rode away from the pines. His range of vision was less than a hundred feet, he reckoned, making it doubly dangerous to ride blind faster than a walk. He heeled the gelding forward, piercing the sheets of windblown water with his eyes, wondering if caution demanded that he draw his gun before proceeding any farther. A few yards from the pine grove he opened his duster and pulled out his .44. Raindrops pelted the gun, his coat and hat, and the golden-yellow hair of his horse, until the animal shook its head to drive water from its ears. "You ain't gonna drown," he said absently to the dun, irritated briefly by the rattle of the bit and curb chain. He examined the darker shapes of trees ahead, slowing the horse to a crawl until he was sure they were pines, not men.

Relying on a vague sense of direction, he continued west until the angle of the ground changed, beginning a steeper climb. The dun plodded up the soggy slope, past trees shedding torrents of rainfall, then open stretches where water cascaded down from above as though Will was riding up a shallow stream. Thunder boomed above his head, rumbling away to his left; south, if Will had guessed right about his direction. Higher up the gelding blew water from its muzzle and shook its ears again, flopping its water-soaked black mane against its neck, rattling the bit.

A muffled pop came suddenly from a spot in front of the horse, and the dun shied, snorting, flicking its foxlike ears toward the sound. Then a crack followed, a noise like splitting wood. Will raised his Colt toward the sound and tried to calm the dun. "Easy, hoss," he said, peering into the wall of gray rain. Was that a gun? Muted by the splatter of raindrops and the distance, he couldn't be sure. When he felt the dun relax between his knees, Will touched its ribs with a spur.

Less than a hundred feet farther up the slope, he came to a tall pine tree blocking his path. A limb was hanging limply from the trunk of the tree, and there was the smell of burning wood. Bark had peeled away where the limb was broken off, revealing a span of pithy white core. Lightning had struck the tree, the popping noise he'd heard moments before. His hand relaxed around the pistol grips. He'd been ready to shoot a pine tree, jumpy as he was. He halted the horse near the base of the tree, hoping to get his bearings. He swung a look around, trying to see past the waterspout falling from his hat. A clap of thunder shook the ground beneath his horse. Seconds later a bolt of lightning arced from the clouds, brightening the trees and rocks around him. He used the brief flash of light to scan his surroundings more closely, and that moment revealed a shape standing in the downpour, one that didn't belong in the forest. A hooded form stood beside a small pine tree, the shape of a man. Will was midway into a jump from his saddle before his brain told him what he had seen—a Comanche!

A gun bellowed from the spot before Will tumbled to the ground. Something hissed, then a tree branch snapped behind him. Will began to crawl frantically through the mud and rocks, gripping the butt of his Colt fiercely, trying to glimpse the Indian again in the sheets of water. He heard his dun gallop down the slope, away from the gunshot. Now he was alone, armed only with his pistol, to face the murderous stalking of a Comanche toward his prey. Fear gripped his chest, numbing his arms and legs as he slithered toward the base of the tree to find protection. Half blind from wind-driven rain pelting his face, he almost missed the darker shape moving toward him through the downpour. The shadowy figure seemed to dance back and forth as Will swung his gun sights and tried to steady them. His breathing came in short gasps and he was sure his chest would explode from lack of air.

Now the shape darted left, whirling away like an eerie apparition from a nightmare. Will followed it with the muzzle of his .44 much too slowly, in spite of his best efforts to make a certain kill. The Comanche swerved this way and that, making an impossible target, yet drawing ever closer to the tree where Will lay. The Indian advanced in rapid bursts of speed, changing direction just when Will's trigger finger tightened.

The Comanche was fifty feet away, pausing to bring his rifle up, when Will fired. His Walker exploded, bucking in his fist, launching a spit of yellow light. The roar of the gun filled his ears while he held his breath, watching, frozen to the muddy ground.

The hooded figure jolted, jerking upright, arms spreading the blanket around him like a bird's wings preparing for flight. A rifle thudded to the bed of pine needles at his feet; there was a coughing sound, then the Comanche toppled over on his back.

Will took a deep, shivering breath, staring at the Indian's left foot twitching with death throes. The deerskin boot quivered a moment longer. Will discovered that he was unable to move, still paralyzed by fear, the old fear he'd known at Fort Mason of Kwahadie Comanches. He knew he should be moving to another position, in case there were more Comanches in the trees around him. But right then, watching a dreaded enemy from his past slip closer to death, he found he couldn't move a muscle. He gazed at the warrior through a driving rainstorm, numbed by the sight and by the knowledge of what he'd just done.

Slowly his mind cleared. He took a look around him, blinking raindrops from his eyelids, then came to a crouch, sweeping the clearing around the tree with his gun. Thunder rattled in the boiling sky above him, though he hardly noticed the sound. He was listening to the hammering of his heart and the ragged breaths of air he sought to fill his aching lungs.

When he was satisfied that he was alone among the pines, he started away from the tree toward the fallen Comanche. His boots sloshed through the mud and sodden pine needles, until he stood above the blanket-draped form. The Indian lay still on his back, his foot no longer twitching. But when Will stared into the hood formed by the blanket over the Comanche's head, he found the warrior's eyes open.

Rain pelted the Comanche's cheeks, though he did not blink or change his expression. His dark pupils turned slightly until they focused on Will.

The two men stared at each other, oblivious to the rain pattering down on them. Will saw the coppery face clearly. Something twisted in the pit of his stomach. This was one of the deadly breed of men who had haunted his dreams so long ago, made him doubt himself, question his courage. It was like awakening from a nightmare filled with ghosts and goblins, only to find a real ghost lying at his feet.

"Leon was right," Will said softly, in a voice strangely like that of someone else. "A Comanche ain't all that hard to kill—"

His last words caught in his throat when the Comanche lunged for his legs with the suddenness of a cougar. A knife blade flashed wetly, glistening with falling rain when it appeared suddenly from a fold in the blanket. Will saw the knife coming and jumped backward, at the same time swinging his Colt for the Comanche's snarling face. His finger jerked the trigger reflexively. The boom of the gun sent a jolt up his arm to his shoulder as he staggered back, struggling to keep his footing on the slippery needles beneath his boots.

The Comanche's lunge toward Will's legs halted abruptly when the force of the .44 slug struck his forehead. The crack of splintering bone could be heard above the gun blast. Blood showered from a hole above the Indian's right eye as he was thrown back against the ground. Red droplets fell on the warrior's cheeks as his arms flopped at his sides. Will, panting, swaying to remain upright on uncertain, trembling legs, watched the downpour wash the drops of blood off the Comanche's face.

"You son of a bitch," he gasped, his sides heaving. Rain rattled down on his hat and coat, drenching the gun still leveled on the Comanche. The attack with the knife had taken him completely by surprise, guessing his first shot to be mortal. A bad guess. "I was right the first time," he said later, when he could catch his breath. "These red bastards don't die all that easy."

He looked around again, thinking better of standing out in the open after the shots were fired. Lowering his pistol, he turned away from the dead warrior and trudged off down the slope to look for his horse.

A few steps away from the body, he allowed himself a mirthless grin. An old ghost from his past had been laid to rest. He knew he wouldn't be afraid of Kwahadie Comanches any longer, no matter how cunningly Iron Horse and his renegades fought him in the days ahead. A well-placed bullet could end the lives of the toughest men on earth, with but a single caution—make damn sure of the bullet's placement before the celebration started. Guessing about it had proven to be a risky pastime just now, a mistake he would never make again.

Chapter Thirteen

Treading slowly back down the slope, he halted suddenly when he thought he glimpsed a pair of horses trotting across his path farther down the mountain. The rain obscured most of what he saw, but it could have been horses. He brought his pistol up and crouched, then resumed a careful descent through the downpour, listening to the squish of his boots and the patter of raindrops on his hat and coat. Thunder rumbled distantly overhead. Now and then the skies brightened with electricity, followed by the angry boom of the storm.

"Will!" The faint cry came from his left. He swung toward the voice and hurried downward.

"Over here!" he shouted, worrying that the exchange might draw more Comanches to the spot.

Then he saw horses moving uphill at a trot. He recognized Billy, slumped over his rain-soaked horse, leading the dun. The rifle in Billy's hands covered his advance up the slope, swinging back and forth.

Will lowered his Colt and waited for Billy to ride up to him, casting a wary look at their surroundings. Billy spurred his bay to a lope and galloped up the incline, reining down when he reached Will's side.

"What the hell happened?" Billy asked, tossing Will the dun's reins. "I found your horse wanderin' down this mountain, an' I had the worst figured."

"Ran into a Comanche," Will said, hoisting his weight off the ground to the rain-slick saddle seat. He looked over at Billy. "I left the others down yonder in some trees. We'd better get back down there. Those renegades could be all around us now.''

Billy's head swiveled, checking the trees and rocks around them. "What happened to the Comanche?" he asked when he was satisfied.

"I shot him," Will answered, swinging the gelding around to ride downhill, "but the rest of 'em are liable to be close.'' He tickled the dun with a spur and struck a trot, peering into the gusting rain below. His horse's hooves splashed through puddles and shallow currents flowing down the mountain. Billy's bay slogged along at the rear. Will still clutched his .44, resting the barrel atop the pommel of his saddle while guiding his horse past landmarks he remembered. His close brush with death still lingered in the back of his mind.

They found the tall pines where the others were waiting, and rode toward them when a flash of lightning revealed horses standing below the limbs. Carl was sitting his horse at the edge of the trees with his shotgun aimed toward their approach.

"What took you so long?" Carl asked when Will entered the pine grove and halted his horse.

Will waited for a roll of thunder to die down before he answered. "Ran across a Comanche up yonder," he said, swinging down, relieved to be out of the fury of pelting rain for a time. When his feet rested firmly on the ground, he holstered his pistol and removed a bandanna from an inside pocket of his coat to wipe his face and neck. His fall left him soaked to the skin. Crawling through the puddles had probably saved his life, but now he would pay for it, spending a cold night in drenched clothing.

"Did you kill him?" Carl asked.

Will nodded silently, mopping his brow with the bandanna, remembering how easily things might have gone the other way.

"Makes two," Carl grunted, edging his horse over. "If that old Injun was right about the count, it leaves eight with Iron Horse. I'm likin' the odds a lot better now. We'll be started back to San Antone in a few days, with a piece of luck.''

Will found Leon watching him closely. Leon's eyes batted and his Adam's apple rose up and down in his neck as he swallowed.

"You see any more?" Leon asked, glancing past the trees.

"Just that one," Will said, returning the bandanna to his pocket just as Billy swung down beside him.

"I couldn't find a dry place," Billy said, looking up at the limbs above them. "This figures to be as good a spot as any to wait out the storm," he added. "We'll have cover all around us if those renegades make a move, an' we ain't as likely to drown."

A clap of thunder boomed overhead, then the hiss of steady rainfall returned while Will was thinking things through. The towering pines kept out most of the water and some of the wind. "I reckon we'll stay here," he said tiredly, letting his shoulders sag. His arms and legs felt like lead weights. Just then all he wanted to do was lie down some place where it was dry. He eyed a big pine trunk deeper inside the grove. The bed of pine needles around the base of the tree looked mighty inviting. "Believe I'll rest for a spell," he said, handing Billy the dun's reins. "Real suddenlike, I need to catch a little shut-eye."

He trudged over to the tree woodenly, puzzled by his sudden fatigue. When he slumped against the pine bark and pulled off his hat, he heard soft footfalls coming toward him across the dry pine needles.

Osate knelt beside him, frowning. She had taken the blanket off her shoulders and began to drape it over him.

"No," Will protested softly, feebly, wagging his head. "You'll freeze. I'm okay. I've got this coat . . ."

She was tucking the blanket below his chin in spite of his objections, clad only in the Comanchero's thin shirt, which barely reached the tops of her thighs. He looked down at her slim bronze legs and shook his head again. "You'll be too cold," he whispered, lifting his gaze to stare into her big liquid eyes, fighting off the sensation of drifting toward sleep.

Weakly, he tried to push the blanket away, unable to command his arms properly.

Her face moved closer to his, and she was smiling. "Funny, touch," she said, looking down at his mustache. Then she puckered her lips and kissed him, the way he'd shown her. Her lips were soft, like velvet. As she pulled away, an involuntary smile crossed his face and his eyelids fell heavily, his head resting against the tree.

He was floating lazily toward a sleep fog when he heard the clank of spurs. Forcing his eyes open, he saw Leon bend over to wrap his blanket around Osate's shoulders.

"Go to sleep, Cap'n," he heard Leon say, although his voice was farther away than it should have been. Something nudged his right arm and then his side, a body snuggling against him.

It was the quiet that awakened him, the absence of sound. He opened his eyes and looked up at the trees. The rain had stopped. It was too dark to see much of anything, but he glimpsed stars in the sky where the limbs parted.

He noticed the weight of the girl resting beside him. Her head lay on his right shoulder. Soft sounds, regular breathing, came from her nostrils. She stirred when he drew his shoulder away to stand up.

His muscles were stiff when he reached his full height. Stretching helped, after he added his blanket to the covering over the girl. His first few steps away from the tree trunk pained him some, but he forced stiff legs and aching knees to carry him toward the horses.

"All's quiet," a voice said. He found Carl slumped against a tree at the edge of the pine grove.

Will took a look for himself. Starlight twinkled from silvery reflections on puddled rainwater beyond the camp. "Storm's gone," he said quietly. Glancing over his shoulder, he saw Billy asleep beside a tree trunk, then two more mounds of blankets near the pile of saddles, which would be Leon and Tasa.

"It quit rainin' a couple of hours ago," Carl remembered.

Then a grin parted his lips. "That little Injun gal has taken a shine to you, Cap'n," he said. "She up'n claimed you over yonder . . . balled herself up right next to you. Appears you've got yourself a squaw, if you take a hankerin' fer one."

"Won't be long till dawn," Will remarked, changing the subject quickly, peering at the sky. "Maybe a couple of hours."

"Plenty of time fer you to poke the woman," Carl said. "Nobody has to know. I'll look the other way."

Carl's suggestion made Will angry. "She ain't hardly more'n a girl, Carl," he snapped.

Carl shrugged and turned back to the clearing around the pines. "You didn't look close enough," he replied. "Afore you gave her that shirt, I seen she was old enough to poke."

Will stiffened and set his chin. "Keep those notions to yourself," he growled. "Valdez an' his bunch gave her all the rough treatment she needs. She was just bein' friendly a while ago, when she came over."

Carl grunted. "I reckon you're right about what them Comancheros done to her. Pretty gal like that, they used her hard. She's liable to start swellin' up before spring with a bastard kid. Shame to ruin a pretty woman like that. A god-damn shame."

Will turned away to check on the horses, and to end a discussion about the girl. He didn't want to think about what Valdez had done to Osate, or the likelihood of her bearing an unwanted baby. He told himself that they had saved her from a life of slavery at a Mexican silver mine, probably a whore for the mine operators, perhaps even death when she outlived her youthful beauty. There were worse things than what she had endured while a prisoner of the Comancheros. He put it from his mind, bending down to inspect the hobbles when he reached the horses.

Dawn came clear and cold. Will watched the sunrise while Carl slept, walking slow circles in the shadows of the trees with his rifle. The night had passed uneventfully. Will judged the coming day was not likely to be so quiet.

He looked up the twin black mountains when sunlight bathed the towering slopes. Somewhere up there, he knew, a hate-crazed Comanche and his followers awaited the arrival of white intruders. Iron Horse could count. His previous attempts to halt the Rangers had cost him two men. He would plan his battles more carefully now, for he understood that his enemies were capable fighters. The ride toward his secret stronghold would be a dangerous affair. The first party to make a careless mistake would pay dearly. Will knew he would have to use better tactics than their Comanche foes, something the best military leaders in the U.S. Cavalry hadn't been able to manage. It was an overwhelming task, trying to outthink Comanches at warfare. Staring up at the mountains, Will wondered just how he would accomplish it.

He'll be expecting us up there, Will thought. He knows why we're riding this direction. Iron Horse is nobody's fool. He'll wait until we are very close before he strikes. We can count on the toughest fight of our lives up there. Sure wish Charlie'd sent along some extra men.

Tasa was moving among the horses, removing hobbles. Will put aside all thoughts of the assault on the renegade stronghold for now, to help with the saddling. Sauntering back into the pines, he was sure of one thing—before they began the climb toward the peaks, he must send the pair of Lipans to a safe place.

Leon and Billy carried saddles to the animals, dragging cinch buckles which awakened Carl. Carl sat up and rubbed his eyes, staring blankly around the camp with a scowl on his face. Then Will noticed Osate stirring beside the pine trunk. She yawned and stretched, letting the blankets fall from her shoulders. Will's gaze fell to the rounding of her breasts inside the shirt, then he looked away quickly and hurried over to help with the saddling.

Billy spoke to him while he was cinching the dun.

"What do you aim to do with them?" he asked, inclining his head toward Osate and Tasa.

Will gave it careful consideration before he answered. "We'll find a safe place to leave 'em," he said, tying off the latigo absently, his mind on the woman. "Can't let 'em go any farther, but it might not be safe to leave them here. If we knew their village wasn't too damn far . . ."

Osate was coming toward him, swaddled in her blanket. He made up his mind to ask her if they could find the Lipan village on their own. He watched her walk gracefully across the uneven ground from the corner of his eye.

She halted near his elbow, making a study of his face. Although he felt some regret that he wouldn't see her when he sent them away, he knew it had to be done before any more lead flew.

"Where are your people camped?" he asked, dropping the stirrup leather over the cinch knot.

"How far?"

He'd expected her to point west, toward the territory, but she turned due south and aimed a finger. She frowned and said, "Chihuahua."

It surprised him to learn the Lipans were in Mexico, and it also troubled him. If she and Tasa rode south, they could be riding back to Diente Oro's home range. Unarmed, they would easily be captured again if they encountered the Comancheros. "We've got to find a safe place for you and Tasa," he said, hoping to sound gentle about sending her away. "We're headed up those mountains to find Iron Horse. It'll be too dangerous to let you go with us. You and Tasa must leave. Do you understand?"

She nodded once and turned toward Tasa. Her voice carried across the pine grove when she spoke to him. The old man stood up near one of the horses and came over, a pair of rope hobbles dangling from his hands.

The girl rattled off a meaningless string of words. Tasa gave his answer, sweeping a palm to the southeast. He spoke rapidly now, making signs with his hands.

"Tasa know place," the girl began when Tasa fell silent. "One sun. Place . . . old one watches . . . goats."

"There's a goat camp down there?" Will asked. "Are you sure?"

Osate shook her head. "Old man . . . many goats. Follow track. You see. One sun." She pointed southeast again.

Will wondered how a goatherder survived so close to Iron Horse and his renegades. What kept the Comanches from killing him? "Will you be safe there?" he asked. Would she understand that all he wanted was protection for her and Tasa?

She nodded quickly.

"Hard to believe a goatherder can make it way out here," he said, thinking aloud. "Wonder what kept him from losin' his scalp to those Indians?"

"I thought I saw some goat tracks back where we walked that ledge," Billy said quietly, remembering. "Hard to tell a goat's prints from a deer. Maybe she's right about that goat camp, Cap'n."

Will sighed. "It's about the only option we've got. Can't just leave 'em here, and they can't go with us." He looked at Tasa closely and formed a question. "Wonder if this old man knows how to use a gun?"

"Gun?" It was Osate who asked.

"Yeah," Will replied. "Does Tasa know how to shoot?"

Tasa seemed to understand. He shook his head and pointed to Will's pistol.

"I carry a spare revolver in my saddlebags," Will remarked, turning for his horse. "I'll give it to Tasa, just in case."

Will removed a cloth bundle from the bottom of one saddlebag and opened the wrapping. A Mason Colt conversion glistened with a layer of fresh oil. He opened the loading gate to inspect the shells. When he handed the gun to Tasa, the old man took it, grunted, and hid it inside a fold of his blanket.

"You'd better head for that goat camp now," Will said, taking a last look at Osate's beautiful face, wondering if it would be the last time he ever saw her. "Go," he added gently. "We'll come to that goat camp as soon as our business with Iron Horse is finished."

The girl understood. She bowed her head, then looked up

at him through her eyelashes. "You come?" she asked, hinting at a smile.

"I'll come," he answered softly. "If I'm able."

She took the blanket off her shoulders, offering it to Will, and he was sure he saw sadness in her eyes.

"No," he whispered. "You keep the blankets. You'll need them. Winter's comin' on. It'll be cold."

Osate made a half turn away from him, then she hesitated and reached for his face with the tip of her finger. "Funny . . . touch," she said quietly, touching the bristles of his handlebar mustache, then whirling away toward the horses, moving off in a hurried walk.

He stood at the edge of the pines to watch the pair of Indians ride off to the southeast. That same odd fluttering that he felt when he kissed Osate the first time occurred in his chest now.

Osate turned at the waist just before she rode out of sight, raising a hand to him as the brown mare carried her past a stand of trees.

He returned her wave with a feeling of sorrow, regret. Then he reminded himself that she was an Indian and he turned away.

Chapter
Fourteen

It was arduous travel for horses. Scaling one steep climb after another, Will rode a rough circle around the base of the northernmost mountain, seeking a trail to follow to the top. Sunlight warmed them. In spite of the high-altitude chill, lather formed on their horses' necks and shoulders as the hours passed.

All morning Will had sensed that someone was watching them from above. The feeling was akin to the dull awareness he got when he was catching a cold—not quite sick just yet, but feeling that something was wrong. Nagged by the sensation of eyes on his back, Will kept a steady hand around the stock of his rifle. He and his men were about to engage the enemy, and he meant to be ready for the moment when it arrived.

In a cleft in the mountainside they spooked a small herd of grazing antelope. Will watched their tawny coats ripple with muscle as they bounded gracefully downslope away from the horses, their white tails flagging a silent signal of danger to each other. The sight reminded him of the need for fresh meat, with the supply of jerky low. But they could not risk a gunshot now, even though he knew that Iron Horse was aware of their presence in the mountains.

"I ain't real clear 'bout what we're lookin' for, Cap'n," Carl complained when they halted the horses for rest. "Can't figure why we don't just head fer the top with our guns drawn."

"We're looking for a trail," Will said patiently, determined not to let Carl get under his skin. "Cortez said there was a trail between these two mountains that would take us to the Comanche camp. When we find it, we'll decide what to do about going higher. Iron Horse will be covering that trail, so we'll have to figure another way up. First off, we've got to find the right spot."

Carl's eyes flickered over the slope above them. "This is gettin' on my nerves," he grumbled, palming his saddle horn, muscles bunching and then relaxing in his cheeks. Two week's worth of black beard almost hid his face. The others had taken the time to shave every day or two, but not Carl.

"It's needin' whiskey that's makin' you nervous," Leon remarked softly. "Wish the hell you had some, so you'd quit complainin'."

Carl turned a smug look toward Leon. "I've got every right to complain about this lousy job, partner," he said. "Twenty a month is damn poor pay. I could make more money stealin' chickens, an' I'd be near a saloon once in a while."

"You're too nervous to make a chicken thief," Billy said.

"Wouldn't be," Carl answered, "if I had me some good whiskey when I took the notion."

"Lately, you've got that notion all the time," Leon observed, wearing a grin as he gazed up at the mountain. "Fact is, when you're sober you ain't very good company, Carl. All that bellyachin' is hard on a man's ears. If I knowed how to brew whiskey, I'd drop off this horse right now and cook up a batch, so you'd keep your mouth shut about it."

"To hell with you," Carl snapped, licking his lips. "All you're tryin' to do is make me thirsty."

Will ended the banter when he urged his horse up the face of a rock slide. The dun scrambled to find purchase among the loose stones, obeying the bump from Will's spurs.

"We're supposed to act like a bunch of goddamn mountain goats," Carl muttered, sending his roan up the climb behind the dun. "Worst job I ever had, bein' a Texas Ranger. My maw wanted me to take up preachin' when I was a kid. Wish the hell I'd listened to her back then."

Leon pulled the spare mounts' lead rope until his horse

began the ascent. "Be hard to fill a church house with folks hankerin' to hear the gospel from a preacher carryin' a shotgun," he said, chuckling, looking over his shoulder at the string of riderless horses behind him struggling up the rock slide. "Don't imagine the good Lord would tolerate much of it either. I'd never agree with your maw on that one, ol' hoss. You wasn't cut out to be no preacher. If you was, that devil's brew wouldn't have such a hold on you now."

At the top of the slide Will reined south to continue the big circle on level ground. Widely scattered patches of thin grass lay in the dun's path; Will allowed the horse to snatch quick bites as it carried him along. Now more than ever, he sensed that they were being watched. But no matter how hard he looked at the jagged rock formations higher up, he saw nothing that might have been an Indian. As the hour approached noon, he began to wonder if he were becoming as superstitious as Leon about some things. Was it only his imagination when he felt this way?

Last night's heavy rains made some of the slopes slippery. In places the dun had trouble keeping its footing, stumbling over mud and rocks, iron shoes sliding in spots where slabs of stone were still slick with water. The rain brought a fresh smell to the wind blowing at their backs, a cleaner scent than the dust assailing Will's nostrils since they came to this country.

Once, he looked down and thought about the girl. He told himself that Osate and Tasa were probably safe for the time being. Iron Horse would be kept busy preparing a surprise attack against the Rangers. And since that day Valdez rode out of his canyon hideout, there had been no sign of the remaining Comancheros. Too, he reasoned that the Lipans were wild Indians. They could survive the harsh land, if they were left alone.

"Yonder's something," Billy said, pointing ahead.

Will squinted into the sun's glare. A quarter mile away he saw a threadlike opening between two slabs of lichen-covered stone. He followed a faint line above the opening with his eyes, a mere scar weaving its way up the face of the mountain. "It could be a trail," he agreed. "Something made that trace . . . it ain't natural. We'll take a look." Tilting his head, he examined what lay at the top. "Appears there's a ledge up there. Maybe we found something."

His fingers closed around the Winchester resting atop his thigh before he asked his horse to quicken its pace. From where they were now, he couldn't see the peak. It was entirely possible that the ledge he saw might lead them to a hollow someplace higher up, a slice or a nook where buffalo-hide lodges were hidden from prying eyes.

He kept his eyes glued to the high ledge as they rode closer to the small opening in the black rocks, for the ledge was a likely spot for an ambush from above. He knew he had to figure a way to send one of his men around to the back side of that ledge before they attempted to bring the horses up. It seemed a natural task for Leon and his keen marksmanship. Only a fool would ride brazenly up the narrow, winding trail without making sure the way was clear.

A covey of quail darted away from their horses, soaring on outstretched wings to the next clump of creosote brush. The creosote smell had grown stronger as they rode higher, and now the slim bushes grew everywhere, tops dancing in the north wind like waves across a brown ocean. The sight reminded Will of Galveston harbor during the war, when Hood's forces were assigned the duty of escorting wagon-loads of cotton to the wharfs before the Union blockade tightened. But here the waves were dry bushes, thick enough in places so they would hide a man lying in wait for his enemy.

"Let's ride up careful," he warned when they were very close to the break in the rocks. "This brush is gettin' thicker. Makes me uneasy, not knowin' what's behind it."

He swung around in the saddle and spoke to Leon. "Give Carl those lead ropes. Take your rifle an' climb around that opening. Make damn sure there ain't nobody waitin' for us, then climb up to the back of that ledge. Looks like a perfect place to take some pot shots. From here on out we move real slow. Those Comanches won't let us march right up to their doorstep. They've planned a little surprise for us, and I don't aim to ride blind. May take us an extra day or so, but we go up cautious.'' He examined the faces of the other Rangers then. ''From here on, kill anything that moves, men. Don't wait to find out what it is. Shoot if it twitches or makes a sound. We'll worry about makin' the identification later.''

Hearing this, Carl actually smiled. ''Mighty damn glad to hear you give that order, Cap'n,'' he said, swinging his duster open so his Greener was free of the coat. ''Me an' little Betsy here are gonna turn some Comanches into fish bait. Hurry up, Leon. Get your ass up there so we can start killin' Injuns.''

Leon dropped off his horse with his rifle. He nodded to Carl and started toward the opening, batting his eyelids furiously. ''I'll see if'n I can scare up a few of 'em for us, partner,'' he said over his shoulder, spurs clanking over rock. ''Just make damn sure you don't aim that shotgun my direction if a redskin jumps up. Wait till I've had the chance to get clear.''

Will watched Leon stalk toward the opening in the rocks. His approach would give him a clean view of what lay beyond. If the brush and rocks were empty, Will would wave Leon higher for a circle around behind the ledge. Just now Will wouldn't have given a gambler any odds at all that the silence around them would continue. He scanned the wind-tossed brush on both sides of the opening, fully expecting to hear the sudden rattle of gunfire.

''Wish he'd taken off them spurs,'' Billy muttered, watching Leon creep higher. ''Couldn't make much more noise if he was beatin' a drum.''

East of the opening Leon crouched and seemed to be wary of something beyond the rocks. Will's arms tensed, holding the Winchester to his shoulder, wondering what gave Leon pause. Seconds ticked away while Leon remained in his crouch. Wind rustled the dry brush, flapping the Rangers' coattails.

''He sighted somethin','' Carl said quietly. ''He's fixin' to start pourin' hot lead at whatever it is. . . .''

Very slowly Leon brought his rifle to his shoulder and

peered down the sights. He took a cautious step forward, then another.

"All hell's about to break loose," Billy whispered, hard to hear above the rustle of creosote branches. Now Billy raised his rifle toward the rocks, closing one eye.

Leon inched forward again on the balls of his feet, hunkered down like a cat about to spring. As he raised a boot to take one more stride, something made him flinch. Before his boot fell, his rifle exploded with a crack.

A squeal came from the rocks. Will's trigger finger had begun to close when a small brown javelina pig bounded through the opening, squealing again, leaving a trail of blood behind. The wild pig ran a few steps more and tumbled to the ground on its chest, its feet kicking. The wounded animal thrashed, making softer grunting noises now, lying on its side in a pool of red.

Leon straightened up from his crouch and shook his head. "I couldn't tell what it was," he called down, wearing a sour expression. Then he swung a look upward, to the ledge. "I'll go 'round," he said with his back turned, wheeling to begin the climb.

Will lowered his rifle. Billy was grinning when Will looked his way.

"They know where we are now, Cap'n," Billy remarked, resting his rifle across his lap.

Will glanced around them, then back to Leon's slow progress up the slope. " 'Spect they already knew," he remarked offhandedly, his attention focused on the ledge. "If I'm any great shakes as a guesser, Iron Horse is watching us right now. Probably havin' a good laugh over that pig Leon shot."

"The sumbitch won't be laughin' much longer," Carl growled, saying it around gritted teeth. "I'll wipe that grin off his face soon as he shows hisself."

Leon began a wide swing through the creosote to go around to the back of the ledge. A gust of wind whistled past the side of the mountain, bending the brush, tossing the horses' manes and tails. Will fixed his gaze on the rim and let his eyes wander back and forth along the rock. No answering fire had followed Leon's shot, making Will wonder if the faint trace up the slope might only be a game trail to higher elevations and not the pathway to the Comanche hideout.

Leon crept to the western edge of the rim and straightened to peer beyond it. Will saw the Ranger's muscles relax. There was no danger behind the ledge. The way was clear.

Leon waved them up and let his rifle dangle at his side.

"Let's go," Will sighed, heading the dun toward the opening where the dead javelina lay. The horse snorted when it scented blood, and on its own stepped wide of the pig to scramble between the boulders. With a mixture of feelings Will rested against the back of his saddle while the dun made the ascent to the ledge above the trail. It was a relief to find that no ambush awaited them here. But at the same time, he had hoped for a discovery that might bring them closer to the renegade stronghold.

His dun struggled over the lip of the ledge to a wide expanse running several hundred yards to the beginning of the next slope up the mountain. Brush dotted the level ground, swaying in the winds. A lone pinion stood near the base of the incline. Leon was standing beside the tree, looking at something dangling from one of the branches. Until Will rode over, he couldn't make out what held Leon's attention. But when the dun trotted up to the windblown pine, he quickly recognized the grisly object. Muscles knotted across Will's stomach.

A human head swayed back and forth in the wind, dangling from a piece of rawhide cord tied to the branch. Even drained of all its color, Will recognized the face. Old Tasa stared sightlessly across the ledge, his pale lips forever frozen in a silent scream. Will watched the Lipan's head swing pendulumlike on currents of air, then he closed his eyes and bit down hard.

"Means they've got the girl," he whispered, more to himself than Leon. "They must have been waiting to jump them someplace when they rode off this mornin'. Damn!"

"Hell of a sight," Leon said softly, still watching the arc of the head as though he hadn't seen enough of it.

Carl and Billy rode over with the spare horses and Leon's gelding. Will did not turn around or open his eyes, thinking about Osate in the hands of the Comanches, wondering if she might also be dead now, a death sentence he'd given both Lipans.

"Jesus," Billy sighed. "That old man . . ."

Will reined his horse away from the tree. Only then did he open his eyes, staring blankly across the distance to the second of the pair of black mountains. He took a deep breath and tried not to think about Tasa or the woman. Not until his stomach settled. It wasn't that he didn't know about Comanche cruelty, their mindless rituals with the bodies of dead enemies. He'd seen their handiwork up close, though it had been long ago, almost long enough for him to have forgotten the savagery of the mutilations.

"He was just a shriveled-up old man," Carl said evenly. "Cuttin' off his head like that don't make any sense."

"I reckon it makes sense to a Comanche," Will remarked, wishing he was someplace else right then. "It's Iron Horse's way of tellin' us he's expecting us up here. He's tellin' us he's ready."

Carl edged his horse over to Will's. There was an odd gleam in Carl's eyes when he spoke. "I know you're grievin' over what could happen to that pretty gal, Cap'n," he said, his voice turning thick with menace, "but if you'll quit all this pussyfootin' now and turn us loose, I'll make that red bastard pay for what he done here." Carl shook his shotgun in Will's face, with his lips drawn back to expose his teeth. "I'll splatter that Injun's head all over creation," he hissed. "I say it's time we quit messin' around!"

Chapter Fifteen

Haunted by a recollection of Tasa's face, Will led his men back down the mountain. Leon cut the knot holding the Lipan's hair and piled rocks around the head before they left the ledge, though Will hadn't watched it, still gazing off the precipice, trying to push the sight from his mind. He knew it was a mistake to let emotion enter his quest to find the renegades. But just now boiling rage welled inside him. Clamping his hands around the reins, he struggled to control it. Like Carl, he was tired of messing around, always nipping at the Comanches' heels.

"We'll ride up that other mountain," he said when Billy halted his horse near the javelina carcass.

"It'll be dark soon," Billy replied, eyeing the setting sun, now a crimson ball hovering above the western horizon. The sun cast a pinkish glow over the mountains, bathing the slopes with blood color.

Will wondered if red might be a fitting hue for what was about to happen here. It was almost certain there would be bloodshed. It would increase the risks to look for Iron Horse in the dark, but in the black mood he found himself in, he knew sleep wouldn't come if they found a campsite to wait out the dawn. Too, a voice inside his head told him it was safer to keep on the move tonight, if they did it carefully. Staying in one place would give the Comanches a chance to creep up on them. Continuing the search in darkness would be fraught with danger, though perhaps only slightly less than sitting still. "We'll stay on the move tonight," he told Billy after some contemplation. "I can't get comfortable with the idea of laying low till sunrise. Those Indians know every foot of this territory. If we sit still, they'll come for us in the dark.''

"Building that campfire at the spring didn't work," Billy reminded him. "Soon as they got close enough to see our horses weren't there, they knew it was a trick an' set out to flank us.''

An idea flashed through Will's brain, listening to Billy's remark. He straightened in the saddle, sweeping the low ground for just the right spot. "That was it, Billy," he said softly, excitement creeping into his voice. "It was our horses that tipped them off. No horses, no white men at the spring.'' He allowed a brief silence to pass. "If we use our horses as bait, we stand a chance of luring Iron Horse down from his hideout. A Comanche's mouth starts to water when he thinks about stealin' horses. If we made it look easy for them to steal our mounts, they'd be tempted. Bait, Billy! That's what these broncs are. Iron Horse will know that if he puts us afoot we'll be easy to kill.''

Billy's face was a mask of concentration, studying the land between the two mountains. "Findin' the right place will be the trouble," he said thoughtfully. "We'd have to have some damn good cover, maybe catch 'em in a cross fire. . . .''

. Measuring the sun, Will knew they had precious little time to find what he wanted in daylight. He began to think things through aloud just as Carl and Leon rode up beside him. "If we can find a place where there's grass, so it'll look natural for us to graze our horses there," he began, "then soon as it gets too dark to see, we spread out around our mounts. Build a fire in some rocks close by and pile blankets over our saddles, so it'll look like we're asleep. Keep that fire small in a circle of stones, so it won't look like we wanted anybody to see it. If we work it just right, they'll make a try for our horses. Comanches get greedy when it comes to horseflesh.''

"I like it," Carl said flatly. "Just lead the way, Cap'n. We ain't got much time to get that trap set whilst we can see.''

Leon was staring off, his face a blank. "We can use that stinkin' creosote brush," he said, as though he remembered something. "When that pig started movin' around, I couldn't tell what it was, them bushes was so thick. If we hid in some

of that brush around our broncs, nobody'd know we was
there in the dark.''

"Let's start lookin'," Will said, urging his dun down the
slope. Down in his gut he was sure the plan would work if they
could find just the right lay of the land. Some of the anger he
felt earlier flowed out of him. Cold determination came in its
place. Iron Horse couldn't resist an opportunity to steal the
horses of his enemy. But Will knew they had to cleverly dis-
guise the real reason behind the night camp they prepared.

Off to the southwest, at the base of the next mountain, a
ridge of jagged rocks formed a hump above the ground. Will
aimed his dun for the spot, worrying that fading daylight
would disappear before he had the chance to look things over
carefully. When the slope lessened beneath their horses, he
spurred to a ground-eating trot. He gazed across the distance, wondering if the mound of boulders might be where
Iron Horse made a fatal mistake.

Soft firelight flickered inside the circle of stones, making
shadows dance faintly on the surfaces of dark boulders around
the three-sided pocket carved into the rock. Stars filled the
sky like a thousand tiny beacons, shedding pale light over
the ridge and the mountains rearing high above the formation. Crickets chirped in the darkness from the brush-choked
flat where the horses grazed. All seven animals moved hun-
grily over the dry bunch grass, restrained by their hobbles to
slow, awkward hopping. The sounds of grass being torn off
at the roots followed the herd, along with the softer noises
of chewing, membranes rattling in velvety muzzles now and
then, and the click of an iron shoe striking rock. The horses
were two hundred yards from the pocket where flames
brightened the ridge. The smells of wood smoke mingled
with the harsh scent of creosote. The winds died at sunset
and the air was still. To further convince the Indians that the
Rangers were camped in earnest, a small smoke-blackened
coffeepot bubbled quietly at the edge of the fire, giving off
the aroma of boiling coffee beans. Three blanket-draped
forms rested just beyond the meager circle of firelight. A

flat-brim hat peered over the top of a boulder overlooking the campsite, as though a sentry watched his surroundings.

Will was satisfied with their preparations. He lay beside a slab of stone with his spare shirt covering the barrel of his Winchester to hide the gleam of gun metal. His belly-crawl through the brittle stalks of sun-dried creosote to reach the rock had been, of necessity, painfully slow, requiring patience and great care. His position made him a rear guard of sorts, slightly higher and farther away from the horses than the rest of his men. It fell to him to prevent Indians from slipping up behind Carl, Billy, and Leon. They were hidden in the thickest stands of brush, forming a crude circle around the herd, with orders to keep moving along with the horses, crawling snakelike without giving their positions away.

When he'd finally laid out the plan, he had known just how great the risks were. Outnumbered two to one by stealthy Comanches, they must above all else prevent the Indians from making off with the animals. No matter what happened, saving the horses was the primary concern. The bait for Will's trap might lure the Comanches down from the mountain, but they must not be allowed to take any of the bait. Should the ambush thin the ranks of the renegades, the Ranger objective would be met. But every last man understood that a Ranger without a horse in this land was buzzard food.

Time seemed to crawl while Will lay motionless beside the rock. He strained to hear every sound from the night, examining every dark shadow as if his life depended on it. His life, and the lives of his men, rested on the success or failure of one man's idea; his idea, a desperate plan at best when pitted against the most cunning warriors on the western plains. Had he been a fool to think it might work?

Now and then he lifted his head to peer over the rock cautiously and scan his surroundings. An hour passed, then two. The fire died to glowing embers. Their horses were moving farther away from the formation, nibbling grass, making Will's job more difficult unless he moved away from the stone himself, keeping the herd within rifle range. His

nerves were on edge. Had the plan failed? Was Iron Horse
too smart to leave the safety of his mountain hideaway?

One more hour passed uneventfully, worsening the drain
on Will's patience, lengthening the distance to the grazing
horses. He knew he had to move now, to protect his men
hidden in the brush.

A horse snorted suddenly in the herd. Billy's bay raised
its head toward the mountain, cocking its ears back and forth.
Again the gelding rattled through its muzzle, still looking at
something up the slope.

"That bay hears somethin'," Will whispered to himself.
Maybe there was a smell. Billy had always shown a prefer-
ence for range-bred horses with a strain of mustang blood,
insisting they were better than a watchdog when a man was
on the move through unfamiliar territory. It was true that
mustang ponies had a keener eye for rattlesnakes lying near
a trail. But the little horses had less speed than good remount
thoroughbred stock. Crosses made better animals. Billy selected only colts bred on open range, claiming wild instincts
were stronger. Now Billy's bay gave evidence that his pref-
erence was a wise choice. The rest of the herd grazed peacefully, yet the bay remained wary of some unseen thing, as it
had when the Rangers had almost ridden headlong into a trap
set by Iron Horse west of the spring.

Will edged his rifle up, resting the butt plate against his
shoulder. His clean shirt formed a tent below the barrel which
hid the metal from starlight. When he thumbed the hammer
back, the click silenced a cricket near his elbow. For a time
the quiet was absolute around his hiding place.

A shadow moved in the brush near the horses. The tops
of bushes swayed, then went still. The movement might have
been made by Carl, coming from the south side of the herd.
Muscles tensed down the length of Will's body as he swung
the muzzle of his rifle.

The creosote moved again; this time he was sure of it. Will
drew the shirttail off the sights and sighted in on the spot where
brush swayed. He heard the bay gelding rattle another warning.

His finger curled around the cold iron trigger, halting before the right amount of pressure dropped the hammer on a cartridge.

A muffled blast erupted in the brush, and all at once horses were moving, lunging away from the explosion. A garbled cry arose from the darkness near a bolt of orange lightning stabbing through swirls of shredding creosote. The concussion produced by the Greener bounced back from the mountain face as a second wave of deafening noise. Then a rifle barked from the brush to the east of the milling, frightened horses, spooking the terrified animals in another direction.

The cry of the wounded man outlasted the gunshots, becoming a wail floating shrilly into the night sky. Will sought a target in the brush and found nothing, only dimly aware that Carl made no shout to announce his first victim in the fight.

A Winchester cracked twice from the north. Lead whined through the air, followed by a pair of soft thumps. Then a gun roared from higher up the mountain. Will jerked his sights to the dying muzzle flash and fired.

The kick of the gun against his shoulder rocked him back in spite of the boot toes he'd buried in the ground. Working the lever, he was momentarily blinded by exploding gunpowder, and his ears hurt. Now guns began to rattle from every direction, the thud of rifles and the scream of speeding lead. Will found the flash of a gun on the slope and nudged the trigger again.

Someone was running toward the horses while Will ejected a spent shell from the chamber. A man darted back and forth, hunkered down to present as small a target as possible. "No!" Will cried, in a voice louder than he intended, whirling to bring the muzzle to bear on a racing figure he could barely see. If the Comanche reached the horses, he would have a place to hide, using the animals for cover.

The Indian was cut down by a wall of sizzling buckshot emanating from the bushes in front of him. A mighty roar accompanied the ball of flame that swept the Comanche off his feet as though he'd run into the pathway of a speeding locomotive. Will blinked when he found his gun sights empty. No trace of the running man remained.

A gun popped, the smaller voice of a pistol on the north side of the swirling horses. Someone shouted with pain and the handgun chattered again, silencing the voice.

Rifle fire crackled from widely scattered spots. Flashing light danced back and forth from the mountain and the brushy flat. One rifle spat six times in succession near the black outlines of lunging horses. Someone whooped amid the melee, a sound that was out of place where deadly guns pounded out a staccato of hissing lead.

Carl's shotgun belched flame, much closer to the mountain than before, muting the rifles with its thunder. Brush swayed in the trajectory of flying buckshot and someone shrieked. Carl was strangely silent. Will could only guess that he didn't want to give his position away until he could claim the highest body count.

Guns boomed in unison from the horse herd and the slope. Will followed a shadow away from one brief muzzle flash, steadying his Winchester until he was sure of the shot. When the Winchester banged into his shoulder muscles, he tried not to blink. He was certain that the shadow faltered. When he blinked and looked again, the shadow was gone.

Now the shooting from the side of the mountain slowed to only an occasional shot, and the rare muzzle flashes were moving farther away to higher positions. Listening to the rifles, Will counted no more than three. In the dark, finding one of the targets was an impossible task at this range, thus he waited, until a lone gunshot brought him scrambling to his hands and knees.

One of the horses whickered in agony and tumbled to the ground. Will knew what that single shot meant—a change in Comanche tactics. One of the sharpshooters was trying to kill off as many of the Rangers' horses as he could, when it became clear the attempt to steal them failed. The horses made big targets for a rifleman high on the slope, and it was only a matter of time before all of them were killed.

Will jumped to his feet and started running. "Get to the horses!" he cried, certain that his voice would draw the Comanches' fire. He dodged back and forth, racing toward the geldings. "Get 'em out of range!"

The thump of his boots and the rattle of spurs quickly caught the attention of a Comanche. A rifle barked on the mountain. Will felt a slug whisper past his face. He ran harder, hands clamped to his rifle, then the gun sounded again. A bullet popped when it tore through his coattail flying behind him. He dove for the ground and went sprawling on his chest among the creosote bushes.

A rifle opened up not far from where Will lay. Five shots rang out. A distant gun answered, then a horse bellowed with pain and there was a thumping noise when the animal fell, and the dry snap of creosote stalks.

A gun crackled to life near the swirling horses, firing once, then again, and a third time. Somewhere high on the slope a man groaned, then a rifle clattered among the rocks.

One final shot echoed off the mountain. The singsong whine of lead ended with a harmless whack in the brush. Will rolled and came up in a crouch, covering the black mountain with his Winchester.

Frantic hoofbeats settled behind him as he gazed up at the slope. A wounded horse grunted somewhere in the dark. Panting from his run, Will tried to steady his hands. The bullet ripping through his duster left him badly shaken.

Something stirred in the bushes. "They pulled back, Cap'n," Carl said hoarsely, moving in Will's direction. "No guarantee the ones we shot are dead. It'll pay to be careful." Carl continued his slow approach to the spot where Will crouched in the brush, the outline of Carl's hat rising above the tops of the bushes. Will said nothing until Carl crept over to him.

"They got two of the horses," Will said quietly. "At least two and maybe more."

Carl made a sound like he was clearing his throat. "If they shot that good roan horse of mine, I'm gonna be mad about it," he replied tonelessly, as though his mind was on something else.

Will hadn't been listening closely, wondering about Leon and Billy. With all that lead flying back and forth, it would be a streak of luck if all four Rangers escaped unharmed.

Chapter
Sixteen

They found Billy seated in the brush, nursing a gaping wound in his side. Billy was fighting the pain, his face drawn, when Will knelt beside him.

"How bad is it?" Will asked in a whisper, opening Billy's coat to inspect the damage, fearing the worst. The closest doctor was a hundred miles to the north at Fort Davis, across impossibly rugged land. Billy would never survive the journey if the wound was serious.

"Grazed my ribs," Billy answered, tight-voiced, wincing when Will touched the bleeding gash in his skin.

Flesh had been peeled away from the pathway of the bullet, and the five-inch tear hung loosely at the bottom, filled with blood.

"Bone turned the slug," Will remarked, tracing a fingertip along one of the exposed ribs. "Looks bad, but I don't reckon it'll kill you. I've got a needle and some thread in my saddlebags. I can sew the flap of skin back. It's gonna be sore as hell when it festers, but it'll heal." He looked into Billy's eyes "Damn glad it ain't any worse," he added softly. "You had me worried."

Billy nodded, his features still pinched. "I'll make it," he groaned, then he swung a look around. "Where's Leon?" he asked, concern softening his voice.

Carl aimed a thick finger. "Walkin' around out there like a damn fool, makin' sure none of them Injuns can still crawl."

Billy's gaze returned to Will's face. "We lost a couple of horses. Leon's, and one of the spares. I reckon we oughta count ourselves lucky. They was tryin' to get 'em all until Leon opened up at that mountain.''

"I'd say we were mighty lucky, all things considered,'' Will agreed.

The roar of a gun sent everyone whirling toward the sound. As the gunshot faded to silence, Carl chuckled.

"Leon found him an Injun that made the mistake of breathin' out yonder,'' Carl said quietly, wagging his head from side to side. Then he grinned. "The ones I shot won't be needin' any air,'' he added, tapping a finger on his shotgun. "A couple of 'em hollered real loud up on that mountain a while ago, like their britches was on fire. It'll be mornin' before we know for sure how many we killed.''

Billy made a move to climb to his feet, grimacing. Will took the Ranger's good arm and helped him up. Billy swayed until he got his balance, pressing a palm over his wound. "Made me dizzy,'' he said, gripping Will's shoulder for support.

"I'll tie a strip of cloth over it,'' Will suggested, "to stop the bleeding. I'll need daylight to sew the skin. Let's get you to that fire.'' He looked over his shoulder at Carl. "See to those injured horses, Carl. Put 'em down if you have to.'' Glancing up to the sky, he added, "It'll be a while before daybreak. We'll need to keep our eyes peeled. Bring the rest of the horses over to the rocks so we can watch 'em. And be careful. There's liable to be one or two more out there in the dark.''

Carl grunted and turned for the horses. "Won't be much longer,'' he said without looking back. "Not with ol' Leon on the prowl.''

Half an hour later a pistol cracked somewhere in the brush as Will was tying pieces of torn shirt around Billy's ribs. The shot made Will flinch.

"That was Leon,'' Billy assured him, forcing a smile.

Before the first streaks of gray brightened the eastern horizon, the death toll was known. Leon discovered another body on the side of the mountain, bringing the total to seven dead. While Will sewed Billy's torn skin together, Leon went on to describe a blood trail he had followed higher up, evidence that at least one more Comanche had been wounded in the fight. "Just leaves two," Leon had said, "if them Lipans was right about the number. Can't tell if one of them we killed might be Iron Horse. Nobody told us what he looked like. Besides, a couple of 'em Carl shot ain't got faces now, so we ain't never gonna know for sure. That damn scattergun don't leave much."

"We need to find that trail to the top," Will said, knotting the piece of green thread in Billy's side. "Maybe the girl's still alive. . . ."

"I found a trail," Leon remarked, thumbs hooked in his gun belt. "It's way up yonder. Runs plain as day toward the face of that mountain. That's where the blood went. Soon as Billy can ride, we can follow it."

"I can sit a horse," Billy said, while Will wound the bandage around him. "It's gonna hurt some, but I'll manage."

Will tied a knot in the cloth and closed Billy's shirtfront. A fresh pot of coffee bubbled deliciously at the fire, giving off scent. He stood up slowly and put the needle and thread away, then walked to the fire and poured coffee. Beyond the ridge, Carl rested against a rock near the horses. Morning sunlight slanted across the land. Will blew steam from his cup and sipped scalding coffee, thankful to see the raw beauty of another dawn. The deadly gun battle in last night's darkness gave him a deeper appreciation for such things today. He and his men had survived the fight. Billy's flesh wound would heal. All in all, things were stacked to the good side.

He turned his gaze to the towering black mountain and thought about Osate. Was the little doe-eyed girl already dead, like Tasa? They would probably learn her fate when they reached the renegade stronghold. He found himself hoping that they wouldn't be greeted by the sight of yet another head dangling from the limb of a tree.

"Tell Carl to bring the horses around," he said. "Time we got saddled. There ain't much jerky left. Pass what there is around. We'll need to find us a young antelope or a deer pretty soon. If I told the truth about it, I've been short of appetite the past few days. But a man's got to eat."

Leon started out of the pocket toward the horses. Will noticed splatters of dried blood on the tails of Leon's duster and on his boots. "Looks like a feller who works in a slaughterhouse," Will remarked absently. "Maybe now he'll be satisfied for a spell."

Billy's face had gone pale by the time he got to his feet with a cup of coffee. "He earned his keep last night, Will. He kept pourin' lead up that mountain, an' he can hit what he aims at, too. Be hard to find a feller any better at fightin' Comanches. I won't argue the fact that he's addle-brained, but he damn sure pulls his weight when the shootin' starts."

Will nodded thoughtfully, watching Leon enter the horse herd to begin removing hobbles. "That's what I can't explain to Charlie," he said, sighing, remembering times when the major demanded answers for Leon's bloodletting, most recently the fight down at Encinal. "Charlie don't understand what we're up against, most times. To him, it's just numbers on a piece of paper, and when the numbers get too high, he complains about it. Never could make him understand what it's like when we've got our backs against the wall."

Billy slurped coffee and made a face. "Like we was last night, surrounded by Comanche renegades. Hard to find fault with a gent who killed as many of 'em as Leon could. Could be that's one reason why we're still alive this mornin'."

Carl and Leon started back toward camp leading the geldings as Will made a study of the men. "I've said they were both crazy, him'n Carl," Will recounted quietly. "A man who enjoys killin' has to have some empty space between his ears. But like you said, those two made a good show of themselves last night. The claim could be made that what they done was necessary. Wish Charlie'd been here to see it for himself."

When the horses were led to the fire, Will helped with the saddling and packing away their gear. Leon chose a spindly chestnut gelding to replace the horse he'd lost to the Comanche guns. The black Carl rode earlier was the sole spare horse they had. Will was silently thankful that his big dun had escaped a bullet. He'd grown to trust the horse and depend on its stamina and speed.

Leon helped Billy into his saddle and got mounted himself.

"Show us where you found that trail," Will said, swinging his horse over to Leon. "Ride slow, an' don't take any chances. We'd be fools if we didn't expect a bushwhacker up yonder someplace."

Leon started the chestnut up the mountain at a walk, swinging his head back and forth. Fifty yards more and he drew his Winchester to rest it across his lap.

From the north the wind began to build.

It would have escaped the notice of most men. The opening was almost too narrow for a horse to squeeze through, half hidden behind a thicket of stunted pinions at the back of a sloping ledge. But when Leon crept through the break in the rock with his rifle cocked and ready, he discovered a tiny hollow. And three pale buffalo-hide tents near the mouth of a cave. Horse droppings littered the floor of the hollow, though there were no horses there now. The renegade camp was deserted when Leon led Will and the others to the lodges where Iron Horse intended to stay the winter.

"No sign of the girl," Will remarked later, after an inspection inside the tents. Buffalo robes and assorted clay pots had been left behind in the Comanches' haste to leave the mountain. Stores of sun-dried meat hung from drying racks and tent poles above the fire pits inside the lodges. Will paid only passing attention to the crude designs and symbols painted on the sides of the tents, for his mind was elsewhere, on Osate's fate.

"She was here, Cap'n," Leon said, emerging from one of the empty lodges with a navy-blue blanket draped over his forearm. "This is one of our blankets, the one you gave her."

Will examined the blanket briefly and shook his head.

"They've got her, there's the proof of it. Maybe she's still alive. . . ."

Carl had an answer ready. "Pretty as she is, they'll keep her alive so they can poke her, Cap'n. Even a heathen redskin has got natural urges."

Will didn't want to think about it and turned away to look inside the mouth of the cave. Dozens of footprints led in and out of the opening, making Will wonder what was hidden inside.

He stooped to enter the dark hole and inched his way along, wishing his eyes would adjust to the bad light. Then he heard his boots splash through shallow water. Crouching down, he dipped his fingers into a pool at the back of the cave, a seep spring, he guessed, flowing from the rock. This was Iron Horse's water supply, permitting him to stay in the hollow as long as he liked. Military patrols might scour the mountains for weeks while the renegades remained in the well-fortified hollow, until the soldiers ran out of food and water for themselves and their horses. Major Copeland's failures to locate Iron Horse started to make more sense now. This was where the Comanches had disappeared after the slaughter at Lajitas. Had it not been for droplets of Comanche blood leading to the spot, the Rangers wouldn't have found it either. Blood had given the Comanches' hiding place away. It seemed a fitting reward, after the bloodshed on the banks of the Rio Grande.

Will came out of the cave, greeted by expectant looks.

"There's a spring back there," he said, to answer the questioning faces. "We'll fill our canteens and carry water out for these horses. Then we'll start looking for the tracks of those survivors. And the girl."

"Wonder if one of 'em's Iron Horse?" Carl asked. "Maybe he's the bastard who left us that blood trail up here."

Leon shrugged. "What difference does it make, partner?" he asked, gazing around the hollow. "They all look 'bout the same when they're plumb full o' holes."

Carl took down the canteens and trudged into the cave without answering Leon, but with a scowl on his face. Leon ground-hitched his horse and went to one of the tents, seeking a pot or a bowl he could fill with water for the animals.

Billy remained slumped over his saddle, hollow-eyed from the pain in his side. A dark red stain had grown larger around the hole in his shirt. Will supposed the ride up the mountain reopened his wound.

"You feelin' okay?" Will asked when he noticed how pale Billy had become. Most likely, before it got dark fever would turn his cheeks a flaming red when the wound began to fester.

"I've felt better," Billy acknowledged, attempting a weak grin. "It's startin' to throb some. Sure wish Carl had saved some of that whiskey."

Will gave Billy a look of conspiracy. "I've got a pint stashed with my clean socks," he said. "Hadn't thought about it till just now." He walked over to the dun and dug to the bottom of a saddlebag, finally producing a pint bottle of Kentucky bourbon he'd been saving for some special occasion that never arrived. When he gave it to Billy, he heard Carl from the mouth of the cave.

"That's the most beautiful sight I ever saw," he said. "Now, I know Billy needs that medicine worse'n me, but I'd sure be obliged if you'd save me just a swallow or two."

Billy took a drink from the pint, closing his eyes when he felt the burn down his throat. "I'll think about it," Billy said, giving Will a sly wink. "May take me a day or two to make up my mind about it. Hope it ain't all gone before I decide."

"I'd be mighty grateful fer a little taste," Carl implored. "Wouldn't drink much. I'll swear to it, Billy."

"Maybe," Billy replied, enjoying himself and the plea in Carl's voice. "I'll think about it real hard. Let you know tomorrow what I decided."

Carl's face fell. He licked his lips, eyeing the bottle in Billy's fist. "Reckon there's a chance you'd decide any quicker?" he asked quietly.

"I doubt it," Billy answered, with as much seriousness as he could muster. "My brain always did work kinda slow, so my maw said."

"Damn," Carl sighed, deeply disappointed.

Billy tipped the pint to his lips again and drank slowly, making bubbles in the neck of the jug. The sound was a grate on Carl's bad nerves.

"Wish I'd been the one to get shot," Carl grumbled. "I'd take a bullet right now, to have just one good drink."

Billy could contain himself no longer. Depsite the ache in his side, he burst out laughing, holding a palm over Will's stitch work until his laughter was spent. "You sound so damn pitiful that I've made up my mind sooner'n I thought, Carl. Come over an' have a drink or two. Listenin' to your begging made my ribs feel better. Get them tears outta your eyes an' hurry over here before I change my mind an' drink all of this myself."

Carl hurried toward Billy like a thirsty man sighting a pool of water, dropping the forgotten canteens in his haste. Will couldn't help but laugh over Carl's eagerness. Only later did he wonder if his laughter might have been the product of relief, when it appeared the battle with Iron Horse was finished at the double mountains. Two more renegades were still on the loose, one with a mortal wound, and they had the girl as a prisoner. But Will liked the odds a hell of a lot better now. The scales were tipped in the Rangers' favor, a rare occurrence for the men of Company C. If he could only rid himself of worry about Osate. . . .

Chapter
Seventeen

The crackle of flames licking up the sides of the tents was a satisfying sound. Will watched the fire consume the designs painted in reds and yellows—a running buffalo, a rising sun, some he did not recognize. A thick black smoke cloud curled into the sky, bending sharply to the south when it lifted above the rim of the hollow into a stiff wind. Wherever the two surviving renegades might be now, they would see the smoke, understand its meaning. Burning out the Comanche stronghold was very necessary, but it also sent the pair of survivors a clear-cut message that this was a victory for the Texas Rangers.

Leon had shown Will empty boxes of cartridges for the Winchesters and Colt pistols found with the dead. There were sacks of flour and dry beans in one of the tents, no doubt some of the booty taken during the Lajitas raid. Flames were destroying everything now, the dried meat and berries, stores of nuts and yamp roots, the entire winter storehouse of food. If the Indians came back, they would find only charred remains. As Will gazed at the fire, a grim smile lifted the corners of his mouth. "We whipped you, Iron Horse," he said thickly, hands shoved in the pockets of his duster.

He turned for his horse and mounted slowly, taking a last look around the renegades' secret hiding place. Then he reined the dun toward the opening and rode between the walls of rock, careful not to bump a knee while his horse squeezed through. The pinions sheltering the niche swayed in gusts of cold wind when he urged the dun to a trot down the slanting ledge to the steep drop in the trail. Will buttoned the front of his coat and turned up the collar, tilting his hat brim. He found he couldn't push the Indian girl from his mind as he started down the mountain. Nagged by visions of what the Comanches might do to her, the satisfaction he felt earlier while watching the tents go up in flames was soon gone. Somewhere in the windblown Christmas range around them, Osate faced the torment of her Comanche captors alone. Burdened by this black thought, he led his men down the mountain in a moody silence.

Billy found the tracks of unshod ponies just before sundown. He counted many sets of prints, and before Will reasoned things out, the number worried him.

"They took all the horses with them," he said later, thinking aloud, following the direction of the tracks with his eyes. "The two that got away drove the rest of the horses off. I suppose they didn't want to leave us anything we could use."

"Here's some blood, Cap'n," Leon said, pointing to the ground from the back of his horse. "The wounded Injun's still bleedin' like a stuck hog. Won't be much fight left in a man who's hurt bad. Leaves us just one to worry about. These tracks head south. I'm bettin' they're headed fer the river . . . maybe to look for Gold Tooth so's they can join up with him. If they cross that river into Mexico ahead of us . . ."

Leon didn't have to finish his thought. All four Rangers understood what that Rio Grande meant to Texas lawmen.

" 'Bout all we can do is push hard after 'em," Will said, looking south in fading daylight, wondering about their chances of catching up before the renegades crossed the Mexican border with the girl. It would be a dark ending to a successful campaign if the Rangers were forced to abandon the manhunt at the river. Valdez would be smart enough to know what the Rio Grande meant, but would the Comanche renegades? "Won't be the first time that river has turned us back."

"It's plumb stupid," Carl complained. "There ain't nobody way out here who'd know the difference if we crossed it, Cap'n. We could ride over an' blow the sorry sumbitches away and nobody'd ever know we done it.''

. ''We would know,'' Will answered softly. ''We took an oath to uphold the law, and the law says we can't cross that river. If that's where these tracks take us, it's the end of it.''

''This is the shittiest job on the face of the earth,'' Carl muttered unhappily, looking to Leon for support. ''We earn a lousy twenty dollars a month with our hands tied. I'd sooner be cleanin' out spittoons in a whorehouse.''

Leon glanced at Will, then his gaze flickered elsewhere. ''We get paid to take orders, Carl,'' he said tonelessly. ''Cap'n Dobbs orders us to turn back, I'll follow them orders. I may not be too happy about it, but that's what I'll do.''

Carl fell into a sulky silence, staring off at nothing. A few swallows of whiskey had done little to soften his disposition earlier in the day, and now the mention of turning back at the Mexican border only worsened things.

''Let's ride,'' Will said, tapping his dun with a spur. ''Won't be long till it's too dark to see these tracks.'' He glanced up at the sky. ''I could use some shut-eye. Tonight maybe I won't be havin' so much trouble falling asleep.''

They rode south into a dusky twilight, four mounted men and a lone riderless horse beneath a purpling sky. The sounds of trotting horses echoed off the slopes around them when they crossed stretches of rocky ground.

Off in the distance, many miles to the south, a coyote howled mournfully at the heavens. Will relaxed against the back of his saddle seat, for the coyote had barked just four times before it wailed.

As he knew they would, the barefoot pony tracks had vanished somewhere in the rocks. No matter how hard Billy and the others looked for hoofprints, they found nothing. Three hours of fruitless search ended at mid-morning when Will signaled the men to ride in. It was pointless to continue riding slow circles any longer. Will knew what the result would be.

"We'll never find them now," he said. "It's no use looking. If they're headed for the border to find Valdez, the best we can do is ride straight south and try to get lucky."

"Remember that goatherder's camp the girl told us about?" Billy asked thoughtfully. His face was red with fever this morning. Last night he slept fitfully as the festering swelled where his skin was joined by the thread. "A man has to figure those Comanches allowed some gent to graze his goats around here, maybe worked a trade for fresh goat meat now and then. If one of the Comanche's is bad hurt like this blood shows, maybe they'd ride for that goat camp to rest up and tend to his wound. It'll be a gamble in the wrong direction if we head east to look for that camp. I've been thinkin' that it was too easy, finding those tracks that took us south. Could be they want us to think that's the direction they rode."

Billy's logic was inescapable. No Comanche, no matter how closely an enemy nipped at his heels, would leave tracks that were so easy to follow. Now that the tracks had disappeared, it was proof enough that the Indians had changed directions. "You're startin' to think like a Comanche, Billy," Will said, looking east. "Osate said the goat camp was one sun away, and she was pointing southeast when she said it. We've been movin' south, so that camp could be real close over yonder. Let's see if we can pick up any goat tracks. Since that big rain, it'll be easier."

"Now we're chasin' goats," Carl grumbled. "Next thing you know we'll be tryin' to catch butterflies." He urged his roan toward Billy. "How 'bout just one more sip of that medicine, partner?" he asked. "I'm startin' to get the shakes."

Billy took the pint from his coat pocket and gave it to Carl. Billy chuckled. "Just a little sip. You ain't the one with stitches."

"I'd sooner be stitched than lookin' for goats without any whiskey," Carl said, pulling the cork to sniff the vapors, a smile on his face now. "Smells better'n fresh-baked bread," he added, then tipped the bottle to his lips with a trembling hand.

With Billy in the lead, they headed east, most often following the contours of low land around mountains. Grass grew thicker where spring and fall rains collected. If there were goats grazing this part of the Christmas range, the animals would be drawn to more abundant grass below the slopes. In places, Will signaled his men to fan out across dry meadows to look for tracks. As the hour approached noon, no one had found a track that might belong to a goat.

Riding out a twisting streambed running southeast, they encountered pools of rainwater, but no prints, as the sun hung directly overhead. Farther east they could see wide canyons feeding toward the Rio Grande. Will judged the river was still two days of hard riding to the south and east. It had begun to look like Billy's idea was costing them valuable time, riding the wrong direction to search for a goatherder's camp that might not exist. They had only the word of Tasa and Osate that someone raised goats in these mountains.

They rested their horses where the streambed forked. A choice had to be made, which direction to follow. Will sat his saddle to study both options, resting an elbow on his saddle horn, frowning in the shadow below his hat.

"Appears we gambled wrong," he said. "If there's a goat in these parts, there ain't no evidence."

Billy was scanning the mouth of a canyon due east of the fork, offering nothing to deny Will's observation. "Maybe we're too far south," he said later, squinting in the glare. "If we don't strike somethin' in the next hour . . ."

Will selected the fork most likely to maintain an easterly course and without comment urged his horse to a walk. The dun's hooves made a clatter over the dry stream bottom, though he paid no attention to the noise. He'd been thinking about the futility of continuing the search for two Comanches in this wilderness of canyons and mountains. Two men who knew the territory could elude a force of a thousand men who didn't know the back trails, the hiding places.

Overwhelmed by the gloomy prospects, he made up his

mind to call a halt to the manhunt at nightfall. Tomorrow they would start back to Diente Oro's hideout and pick up their lone prisoner, Santiago Cortez. What Company C had been able to accomplish would have to be enough to satisfy Major Peoples and Governor Davis. Will's report would list nine Comanchero dead and a live prisoner, plus eight renegade Comanche casualties. A respectable amount of a difficult assignment was behind them, finished, handled by just four Rangers. Even if Iron Horse had survived the gunfight, there would be no more massacres like the one at Lajitas without warriors to follow him. And Will could truthfully report they had broken the backbone of the Comanchero gang, perhaps ending a slave-dealing operation that Charlie and the governor had known nothing about. The report wouldn't make mention of loose ends, like Gold Tooth's escape into Mexico or the pair of Comanches who'd gotten away. Though Will hated paperwork like cattlemen hated sheep, he knew he could write a glowing report listing Company C's activities out here. Backed by three brave men, he'd ridden into the teeth of outsized odds to strike a mortal blow for the state of Texas against lawbreakers.

Down in his gut he wasn't satisfied, however. Osate was still a Comanche prisoner, and Gold Tooth Valdez was still on the loose. It went against Will's grain to leave unfinished business behind. Thus he set his jaw and continued along the streambed

Leon noticed the hard look on Will's face. "What's eatin' on you, Cap'n?" he asked, swinging alongside the dun.

"Just this badge, I reckon," he answered tersely, grinding his teeth together as soon as the words left his mouth. "Charlie sent us out here to get a job done. It don't set well in my craw when it's half finished, but there ain't much more we can do. We'll ride down an' pick up that Comanchero, then head back. Like lookin' for a needle in a haystack, this is."

Leon's flat expression gave no hint of his feelings on the subject until he spoke. "Knowin' Gold Tooth Valdez is likely just south of that river puts an itch in my trigger finger," he said. "I got a look at him whilst I was up on that rim. Big

feller. Wearin' two pistols, he was. That prisoner we took
said Gold Tooth carried two pistols, after I took my rifle away
from his balls so he'd tell me the truth. I swore I'd make a
gelding outta him unless he told me which one was Gold
Tooth. If we could figure a way to get Valdez back on this
side of the river, you've got my word I'll kill him deader'n
pig shit this time.''

Will swung his head back and forth. ''I doubt there's any
way to lure him back to Texas until he knows we're gone,''
Will remarked. ''He knows we can't touch him in Mexico.''

Leon agreed silently, watching Billy trot his horse up the
bank of the wash. Billy was holding his injured side, as
though it pained him.

Billy halted his bay suddenly to peer down at something.

''Up here, Cap'n,'' Billy cried.

Will hurried his horse up the bank to see what caught
Billy's attention. Before he brought the dun to a stop, he saw
the tracks, and the piles of fresh goat droppings.

Then, near the mouth of the big canyon they'd seen around
noon, they heard the tinkle of a tiny bell in the distance.

''That's a lead goat's bell,'' Will said, standing in his stirrups for a better view of the canyon. ''Maybe we've hit pay-
dirt after all.''

The rattle of armament behind Will did not require a look
to find its source. Carl began loading his shotgun. Leon fingered shells into the loading gate of his Winchester, then he
spun the cylinder of his .44, reminding Will to do likewise
before they headed into the prospects of trouble.

Chapter
Eighteen

They rode into a place apart from the barren desert mountains when they entered the mouth of the canyon. What caught Will's eye first were the rows of fruit trees—wild plum and hardy little peach trees like those cultivated along the Pedernales River bottom near Fredricksburg. Other varieties he didn't recognize had been planted in neat rows farther into the canyon, perhaps fist-sized native pear and smaller Mexican orange trees. It was an oasis, even so late in the year, the fruit long harvested. Whoever tended the orchard carried countless bucketsful of water to the trees during the long dry season from May to October. Thirty or forty fruit trees would require almost continual care in the middle of this wasteland.

Spanish goats bleated from sloping sides of the canyon. The ground was littered with goat tracks where Will led his men cautiously toward a small adobe hut inside the trees. A nondescript black dog started to bark from the front door of the dwelling, which brought a man clad in white homespun to the door frame to watch their approach.

"He's got a gun," Carl observed quietly.

"I can kill him from here, Cap'n," Leon said, bringing his rifle halfway to his shoulder.

"Hold your fire," Will ordered, eyes fixed on the gun held loosely in the goatherder's hands. "No reason to shoot him if he's peaceable. Keep on the lookout for that pair of Comanches. . . ."

Will raised a hand in greeting as their horses carried them closer to the hut, continually examining the slender trunks of fruit trees for a place where the Indians might hide. Behind the adobe a pole corral held three rawboned burros. He saw no Comanche ponies in the canyon, no evidence the renegades had sought refuge here.

The shriveled Mexican stepped out in bright sunlight, still clinging to the stock of a double-barrel shotgun. The old man watched the four riders, but made no move to bring the gun up. He said something to the dog and silenced it. Will rode straight for the house, then hauled back on the dun's reins when he was roughly fifty feet away.

"Buenas dias, viejo," Will said, giving their surroundings one more careful look. *"Estoy capitan de los* Texas Rangers. *Habla inglés?"*

"Si," the old man replied, nodding. A slow smile webbed the etched lines of his face. "I speak English, *Capitán. Muy pobre inglés* . . . very bad English. I am Pablo Bustamante. Welcome to my home. Come down from your horses, senors. I have cool water, and dried fruit if you are hungry. And goat meat."

Will remained in his saddle until he knew more. "We're looking for a couple of Indians. One of 'em will be hurt. Got a bullet hole in him. We've been followin' his blood trail."

Pablo bowed his head. "The wounded *Indio* is here," he answered softly, lowering the muzzles of the shotgun to his side, aiming a thumb over his shoulder to indicate the adobe. "Maybeso he is dead now. His wound is very serious, in the stomach. *Dios* will claim his soul very soon."

"Injuns ain't got souls," Carl grumbled. "Comanches ain't human. You'd understand, if you seen what they done to this old man back at that black mountain."

Pablo wagged his head. "All men have souls, senor," he said in the softest of voices. Then he looked at Will. "You are wrong about one thing, *Capitán*," he added, then he fell silent.

"What's that?" Will inquired darkly, with a look around the hut.

"Three *Indios* came here this morning. Two rode away before noon. One was only a girl. Her hands were bound with leather. The other *Indio* is known to me . . . he is the terrible one, Conas Woba-Poke. In English he is called Iron Horse." Pablo made the sign of the cross when he said the name, more proof of the fear in his voice when he identified the Comanche chieftain.

"Did he take the girl with him?" Will asked, knowing the answer.

"*Si* . . . yes," Pablo replied. "She is not of Sata Teichas blood, of that I am certain. Iron Horse treated her roughly, *Capitán*. Her life means nothing . . . to him."

Will felt himself relax. "The one inside is wanted for murder," he told Pablo. "Iron Horse's bunch killed twenty-three people down at Lajitas. We'll have to take the one inside, or make sure he's dead."

Pablo nodded again. He understood. "They are terrible men, the Sata Teichas," he said hoarsely. "I gave them fruit and meat. Because of the food, they did not kill me. Many times the soldiers came here, asking about Iron Horse. Always I said nothing, fearing for my life."

Will gave Carl a look, then pointed to the adobe before he left his saddle. He sighed heavily, stepping to the ground. "They're all dead now, but these two. It ain't exactly good news to learn the one who got away is Iron Horse."

Carl had dismounted ahead of Will and strode purposefully for the hut with his Greener leveled. Will heard the metallic click of hammers being cocked before Carl ducked in the doorway. The black dog growled a warning, until Pablo silenced it again to allow Carl to the entrance.

Will stepped over to Pablo, offering a handshake. Just as the old man took Will's palm, an explosion rocked the hut. The dog yelped and whirled toward the sound. Pablo stiffened and quickly drew his hand away. A horse snorted behind Will, a hoof scraped backward while the sounds of shattered glass tinkled softly to the floor beyond the doorway. With the shotgun's roar slowly fading to silence, he groaned and whispered, "Damn!"

Carl emerged from the entrance with a wisp of gun smoke curling from one barrel of the ten-gauge. "He came up with a pistol, Cap'n,'' Carl explained. "Wasn't nowhere near dead. But he is now. Sorry 'bout the mess,'' he added, speaking to Pablo.

Pablo shook his head that he understood. "He was dying, senor. Perhaps it is the will of *Dios* that he is gone now."

Leon was down from his horse, handing Billy his reins. "I can drag what's left of him outside, Cap'n,'' Leon said, walking to the door to peer over Carl's shoulder.

"Won't be necessary,'' Will said quickly, before Leon went in. "We need to stay on Iron Horse's tracks. Won't be time . . .''

Leon gave Will a puzzled look. "There ain't been any tracks all mornin',''' he protested.

Will set his chin. "Get mounted, Ranger,'' he snapped, suddenly weary of events. He looked at Pablo. "We'd be obliged for some food, maybe some of that goat meat an' dried fruit. We'll pay, and a little somethin' extra for the mess Carl made inside.''

"I had to shoot him, Cap'n,'' Carl protested, hearing the tone of Will's apology to the old man. "He had a gun under that blanket. When I came in, he opened his eyes an' raised that pistol—''

"Never mind, Carl,'' Will remarked sharply, to end a further description of how things happened. He opened his coat and dug in a pocket of his denims, producing a handful of silver coins. "For the food,'' he said, gazing around the orchard when he handed Pablo the money. "Nice place you got here,'' he added, making conversation to take the Mexican's mind off what he would find when he returned to his house. "Never figured to find a fruit grove way out here.''

Pablo pocketed the coins. "I sell my peaches and oranges in the spring,'' he said, "and some of my young goats. The people in Lajitas loved my plums and pears . . . but now, no one is there to buy them, so I must lead my burros to Presidio next year, if *Dios* gives me a good crop in the spring.''

Pablo turned for his hut. "I will prepare the food,'' he said, scuffing his worn sandals to the door. When he looked inside, he made the sign of the cross again and disappeared into the shadows of his house.

Carl walked up to Will, still wanting to explain.

"I didn't have no choice," he said, with a shrug of his broad shoulders. "The sneaky sumbitch was aimin' to shoot me. Wasn't time to bust his skull. It was him or me."

Some of Will's irritation faded. Carl's explanation made sense when Will remembered the Comanche's lunge with a knife during the rainstorm. He was set to agree that Comanches were hard to kill, when Leon came over.

"I'm damn sure hungry," Leon said. "Goat meat beats the hell outta jerky, after a steady diet of dry beef. Peaches sound good too. I've worked up a helluva appetite," he added, evidencing no stomach distress after a look at the dead Indian.

Carl turned a thoughtful stare to the hut. "Wonder if the old man's got any whiskey? Maybe tequila? I'll pay real good for most anything he's got." Carl started for the door, bent on finding a solution for his jittery nerves, until the dog snarled again near the entrance. "Get the hell outta my way, dog," Carl warned. "I said I was willin' to pay for the stuff."

Something about the big Ranger made the dog back away with its tail clamped between its legs, no longer growling. The sight made Billy chuckle. "That dog knows not to fool with a gent who's in a hurry to find a drink. 'Specially not Carl Tumlinson. Proves it's a smart dog, in my opinion. Carl's on the prod an' that cur knows it."

Will swung around to instruct Leon. "Take our horses over to that well," he said, examining a circle of stones west of the adobe. The well explained the survival of the orchard. Without it, this canyon would have been like all the others they'd seen.

Leon helped Billy out of his saddle, then he trudged off with the geldings in tow. Will glanced down at Billy's ribs. "Maybe Pablo has some remedy for the swelling," Will offered. "Let's go in and ask."

Billy shook his head against the idea. "I'd just as soon not look at pieces of that Comanche," he said, adopting a weak grin. "I can wait till he comes out with the food, Will. And knowin' how pale your face gets at times, I'd suggest you do likewise."

Will started for the hut in spite of Billy's warning. "I can tolerate it," he said quietly, wondering if he could. He bent down to avoid the low door frame and stepped inside the tiny adobe, his nostrils wrinkling when encountering blood smell.

Pablo was wrapping a piece of cloth around a mound of smoked goat meat. Even with the stench of blood filling the room, Will could smell the chilis and cilantro used to prepare the meat before it was cooked. Carl stood near the old man's shoulder, admiring a hollowed-out gourd jug with a wooden stopper in the neck, while his hand sought money in his pants pocket. "Pulque," Carl said, when he heard Will's boots. "Pablo makes it hisself, an' he's sellin' me a jug of home-made plum wine too. Sure glad we found this place."

Will tried to ignore the pulpy mass resting against the far wall of the hut. He didn't need to see it clearly, the pellet-torn remains of the Comanche. He waited for Pablo to turn around with the bundle of food. "One of my men's hurt. A bullet cut a gash over his ribs and it's swellin' something awful. Wondered if you had a cure for a festered wound."

"I have a small bottle of herb oil," he answered, glancing to a shelf. "It holds the magic of a *curandero*. I buy it from an old woman in Ojinaga. Pour it over the wound, and the *curandero*'s magic will be revealed in good time." He went to the shelf and took down a small lavender bottle.

Will gave Pablo a silver dollar for the oil and hurried out, to be free of the blood scent. "Here's some sort of magic potion," he said, handing the bottle to Billy. "He said to pour it on the swelling. It's worth a try."

Leon bucketed water for the horses, dropping a sisal rope into the well to refill the wooden bucket. Will inhaled a deep breath of fresh air, watching Leon go about his work.

Carl came outside with the gourd of pulque. Will knew the sour taste from years along the Mexican border and quickly declined Carl's offer of a drink. "Might try some of that plum wine," he said when he saw the corked neck of a bottle in a pocket of Carl's duster. "Maybe tonight, while we rest our horses."

Carl grunted and removed the wood plug from the neck of the gourd. He took a swallow of the milky liquor, then another, and emitted a satisfied sigh. "It ain't too bad," he said, though his tone might be called doubtful.

Billy was pulling his bandage away from the stitches to administer some of the herb oil. A foul smell arose from the lavender bottle when Billy removed the cork.

"That stuff stinks," Carl said, watching Billy apply a small amount of the oil.

Billy made a face. "It don't smell near as bad as that pulque," he said. "I'd just as soon drink a rattlesnake's poison. In the mornin' it's gonna feel like your skull's about to explode."

"You're a sissy," Carl replied, lifting the gourd to his lips again.

Pablo came out, glancing toward the well where Leon was watering the horses. Will had one last question for the old man, for he knew just how well the Mexican knew these mountains.

"That Indian girl's life won't be worth a plug cent unless we can find her," Will began. "Tell us which way Iron Horse went when he left here, and which way you figure he'll go."

Pablo frowned, gazing absently at the mouth of the canyon. For a time he said nothing. "He took her to the south," he finally replied, stroking his chin thoughtfully. "He will ride for Mexico, seeking the evil *jefe* of the Comancheros who supplies him with guns and bullets. The evil one is called Diente Oro, and he will be waiting for Iron Horse just below the border."

Will shook his head. "We had a run-in with Diente Oro. I figure the Rio Grande is two days south. Iron Horse will need water for his horses before he gets there. If there was a spring along the way, he'd ride for it."

"There is such a spring, *Capitán*," Pablo remembered. "I can tell you how to find it. A day's ride closer to the river, you will see a large mesa to the west. The top will be covered with sotol bushes. Ride up the mesa and look for a very large rock surrounded by sotol. Below that rock there is a cavern running down to a spring. The Sata Teichas know this place. It has served them well for many years.'' Pablo turned his gaze to Will and lowered his voice. ''Be very careful, *Capitán*, if you ride to this spring looking for Iron Horse. Of all the *Indios* I have seen in my lifetime, he is the most fearless. He has the strength of two men, and the cunning of a cougar. When I looked upon his face, I could see the fires of El Diablo in his eyes.''

''Never expected him to come quietly,'' Will said. ''We're obliged for the information.'' He lifted a boot to a stirrup and pulled himself into the saddle. ''We'll find him, if he stops runnin' long enough. *Buenas suerte*, Pablo.'' He waved and turned the dun.

''Vaya con Dios,'' Pablo whispered, crossing himself as the Rangers trotted away from the hut. He watched them ride through the orchard until they disappeared beyond the trees where the canyon narrowed.

Chapter
Nineteen

Wind blew at their backs, sweeping the horses' tails across their flanks, swirling dust around them. The land they entered was dry, denied the heavy rainfall that had come to the black mountains. A layer of chalk covered the men and animals. Windswept caliche rolled in great clouds in front of the horses, obscuring what might lie behind the next yucca or mesquite. They'd seen the last pinion when they rode away from the Comanche stronghold. Desert flats and dry canyons stretched endlessly to the horizon before them. A setting sun hung like a flat orange disk above empty land. Shadows fell away from plants and rocks in the Rangers' path, lengthening, growing darker. Will sent a roving eye westward, looking for the mesa bristling with sotol spines. If old Pablo had been right, they would find the mesa tonight, though Will would not risk the climb toward the spring until the following morning, if he had a choice. He worried that Iron Horse would slit the girl's throat when he sensed danger. The Comanche would have to be approached carefully if Osate's life was to be spared.

"Pony tracks, Cap'n," Billy said, halting his bay, aiming a finger to a spot below his horse. "A bunch of 'em. Iron Horse is keepin' those extra ponies with him. Can't figure why, 'less he aims to throw us off when he scatters 'em. Don't appear he's tryin' to hide his tracks any longer. Maybe he's sendin' us another message like he done up on that mountain, tellin' us the direction he wants us to go."

"Don't seem natural for a Comanche," Will agreed, following the trail of prints with his eyes.

"Surely the sumbitch can count," Carl wondered aloud. "There's four of us an' just one of him. Leavin' tracks a blind man can see ain't none too smart. Same as gettin' an invitation to a barn dance. All this time he's been runnin' like a scared rabbit, an' now he shows us where he aims to run, like he wants us to know."

"You can bet your bottom dollar it's a trick," Leon offered, and now he started to blink.

"Comanches are tricky sons of bitches," Carl replied with a flourish of his Greener, "but my maw didn't raise no fool. Soon as I saw that blanket twitch back yonder at the Meskin's place, I showed that Injun a trick or two. Little Betsy carved him up like a turkey hen, Leon. Wish you'd seen it fer yourself . . . there was pieces stuck to the wall, an' that blanket come apart—"

"That's enough, Carl," Will growled, his belly swollen with dried sweet plums and tender goat meat. He didn't want the delicious meal to come boiling up his neck, listening to Carl's description of the killing.

Billy was scowling at the ground. "That's what he'll do, Cap'n. He'll scatter those loose ponies, maybe later tonight. That way we won't know which sets of tracks to follow. By the time we find all the loose ponies, he'll be across that river with Valdez. He's plenty smart. He knows the four of us can't follow so many tracks if they go different directions, not even if we split up."

"Splittin' up's the best plan," Will said thoughtfully. "We'd stand a better chance that way, only we'll be up against him alone, whoever follows the right hoofprints. A lone white man who don't know this country could wind up with his hands full when he meets up with Iron Horse."

"It'd suit the hell outta me," Leon said softly, blinking at the southern horizon as rapidly as his eyelids would work. "We could see who's got the best aim."

Carl grunted his agreement. "Just afore I blowed his head off, I could tell him what I done to his partner back yonder. I ain't worried none if I'm the lucky feller to find him. Been lookin' forward to it ever since we come to this god-awful place.'' Then Carl toasted his luck with a swig of pulque, spilling some of the white substance into his beard stubble.

Will sat his horse a while longer, mulling things over, weighing the risks if the Rangers split up. Billy would be at a disadvantage with his wound, though his cautious nature would keep him from taking chances. Leon was a dead-shot rifleman, but he took foolish risks far too often. And Carl would charge full tilt into anything holding promise of a fight, bravery Iron Horse could use to lure him into a death trap. Splitting up could cost a Ranger's life, something Will didn't want on his conscience.

''Stay on those tracks, Billy,'' Will said, ending his deliberations abruptly. ''We'll see what Iron Horse does tonight. We can decide how we'll handle it when the time comes.''

Billy spurred his bay to the south, his head bent down to see the prints in fading daylight. Will cast a wary glance toward the sunset, then sent his horse forward with a growing uneasiness. The sudden appearance of pony tracks nudged something in the back of his brain. They were in Iron Horse's home range, and now he was showing four Texas Rangers the route he had taken. Comanches didn't do business this way.

They found the first grazing pony some time after midnight. Will ordered a careful approach until they were certain the little horse wandered freely between bunches of grass. The ewe-necked buckskin limped away gingerly when the Rangers circled it, carrying a forefoot, snorting at the unfamiliar smell of white men.

Billy rode over to Will and pointed south. ''Tracks go five or six different directions over there,'' he said. ''This buckskin was too lame to go very far. It's gonna be a job, tryin' to figure which tracks we oughta follow.''

Will eased his sore rump off the saddle seat, standing in his stirrups for a better look at the shadowy land bathed in pale starlight. ''It's takin' a hell of a chance, splittin' up,'' he said. ''Down in my gut, I know he'll head for that spring old Pablo told us about, then he'll ride hard for the Rio

Grande to find Valdez. Still, there's a chance he'll take another direction, to throw us off, maybe buy more time till he figures what to do about us.''

"It's the girl, ain't it?" Billy asked. "You're worryin' about what he'll do to her.''

"No sense denyin' it," Will said. "It's unfinished business, and I never did like loose ends.''

"It ain't none of my affair, but it was real plain you took a liking to her.''

"That's not all of it," Will protested. "We owe that pair of Lipans something. Helpin' us cost the old man his life.''

Billy tented his shoulders. "So what's your idea on how to find her?''

A dangerous plan had begun to take shape in Will's head. If he rode for the mesa alone, he'd be the one taking the risk. Sending the others back down to the Comanchero camp to pick up Cortez made the most sense. They could wait for him there. "I'll head west to look for that spring," he began. "The rest of you head south to that Comanchero hideout to pick up Santiago Cortez. If I run across Iron Horse and the woman, I'll do what I can to set her free. No reason for all of us to ride all over creation lookin' for one Comanche.''

"It'd be smarter to pair up," Billy argued. "I could ride along an' watch your backside.''

Will shook his head against it. "Gold Tooth might be waitin' for whoever rides in. Last count we had, Valdez and three more were still on the loose. I'll go it alone to that spring. Iron Horse is just one man. If I find him, it'll be just me an' him to settle things.''

Leon spoke up first. "Wish you'd take me with you, Cap'n.''

"I'll handle it alone," Will said softly. "Take your orders from Billy till I get back." He gave his men a lazy salute and lifted his reins. "Ride careful. Valdez will be dangerous, if he's down there." As an afterthought he looked at the dark faces around him. "If it works out, try an' take those Comancheros alive. Charlie's gonna throw a fit when I give him my report listing the casualties. Live prisoners might soften him some, somebody the governor could hang just before election time.''

He sent the dun away from the group, certain that Carl and Leon were unhappy over the order he'd given to take Valdez and his men alive, if they could. Chances were that neither Ranger would look very long for the opportunity to capture members of the gang when he was away, tending to other matters. But it felt good to give the order anyway, sounding like a Ranger captain should. From the very first, Will had known about the governor's real feelings. Company C had been sent out here to end a problem any way they could, and Will knew why he and his men had been picked for the job. His company had a reputation for spilling blood. Everyone conveniently ignored the fact that Company C got sent to the worst trouble spots to face men who understood only one kind of law—the law of the gun.

Sotol stalks bristled against a paling dawn sky like a thousand bony fingers aimed toward the heavens. The silence across the mesa made Will doubt his senses. There had been no sound, no movement, during the pair of hours Will spent behind a sotol plant, lying on his belly to await the arrival of daylight.

Finding the table mountain had been easy enough, but the slow climb up the slanted side had required long, watchful pauses where there was cover for the horse. Leading the dun to the top had taken time, and every ounce of stealth he could manage. The gelding's iron shoes rang like warning bells to whoever might be waiting at the top. Tying off the horse down below had been out of the question. If Iron Horse lurked somewhere high on the rim, the Indian would come for his dun as soon as he was out of rifle range.

Thus he'd been forced to wait for dawn, unwilling to chance an approach toward the spring when he couldn't see what lay in store. Now, as gray light brightened the sky, it was time to move. Pushing off the ground, he pulled his Walker. A fight amid so many sotol bushes would be at close quarters, making a rifle too slow. With his hand wrapped around the butt of the `.44, he started forward without his spurs, placing weight on the balls of his feet. He held the dun's reins in his free hand and pulled the horse slowly behind. The big rock Pablo described was somewhere in front of him, hidden by thick sotol clumps and spiny leaves. Will's heart was pounding. He had chosen to turn the tables on a fierce Comanche, stalking him rather than being stalked, all for the sake of a slender Lipan woman he had known a mere handful of days.

The dun's hooves crunched over pebbles, plopping like drum beats on hard ground. Every sound made Will flinch inwardly, for a Comanche's ears were atuned to the slightest disturbances upon Mother Earth. If Iron Horse was waiting at the spring, he would hear his approach and be ready for it. There would be a test of lightning reflexes when they met among the sotol, a battle to the death between seasoned fighting men. Only one would walk away claiming victory, and Will meant for that man to have a star pinned to his chest. If Lady Luck smiled on the winner, his name would be William Lee Dobbs.

He crept forward, then hesitated, cocking his ear, scanning the sotol until he was satisfied. Only a few steps more and he paused again, covering the plants and shadows with a sweeping motion of his revolver. There was no wind to carry sound this morning. When he remained frozen to a spot, the silence around him was absolute.

Suddenly, clear as a bell, a horse nickered somewhere in front of him. Will clapped a hand over the dun's muzzle to keep it from answering another animal. "Quiet, hoss," he whispered. "That was a Comanche pony."

His heart was racing now with the knowledge that Iron Horse was at the spring, as he'd predicted. Had the pony's nicker alerted the Comanche to Will's presence?

Time to move, he thought quickly. Iron Horse would start looking for whatever the pony saw or heard, warned the same way Will had been warned when Billy's bay snorted at the dark mountain.

Will swung a look over his shoulder, then to either side of

his horse. When the dun moved, it made too much noise. But if he left the horse, Iron Horse would claim it, leaving him afoot. The grim choices flickered through Will's mind— abandon the horse, or risk the sound of leading it to cover. A clock was ticking inside his head. The Comanche would be moving closer now.

Will resumed his cautious advance, one footstep at a time, hunkered down in a battle-ready crouch with the Walker aimed at the brush. The dun's hooves made a grinding noise behind him, obedient to the pull on its reins. Will was certain Iron Horse was listening to the telltale sound somewhere close by, awaiting the chance to kill his adversary with a well-placed shot from the sotol. No white man could equal the stealth of a Comanche; a black thought as Will advanced through the dagger-shaped sotol leaves.

He came to an impenetrable wall of spines and halted to raise his head above it. Shafts of golden light brightened the mesa as the sun edged to the horizon at his back. He forced his eyes to move slowly from left to right across the tops of the five-foot bushes blanketing the top of the mountain until he found what he was looking for. A slab of pale limestone rested on its side in a clearing surrounded by sotol, and beside the rock, a sorrel and white pinto pony rested hipshot next to a high-withered brown mare. The horses were two hundred yards from his own hiding place, two hundred of the most dangerous yards he would ever cross. A white man in high-heeled boots leading a thousand-pound horse stood no chance at all of sneaking up on the spring while it was guarded by a Comanche.

Tiny hairs prickled down the back of Will's neck. He could almost feel Iron Horse's presence. Frozen behind the wall of leaves, his mind raced with possibilities. To approach the spring leading the dun would be suicide. Abandoning the horse might mean a slower form of death if he lost the animal to the Comanche.

Before Will could make a choice, the pinto pony lifted its head. The mustang's ears pricked forward and its muzzle flared. Even from so great a distance, Will could hear the warning rattle of the pony's membranes bulging from its nostrils. Will's heart leapt to his throat. The very same feral instincts in wild horses that had cost Iron Horse so dearly at the black mountains now warned him of Will's approach. There was no more time to debate the choices. A deadly game of hide and seek was coming to an end.

A man's head and shoulders appeared from behind the rock, then the glimmer of sunlight on the barrel of a rifle. Will ducked down to make a grab for his booted Winchester, his chest hammering. The split-second glimpse he'd had of Iron Horse confirmed his darkest fears. The renegade chieftain was powerfully built, with an animallike grace when he sprang from behind the stone. Though Will had only a vague impression of the Comanche's face, he was certain the Indian's lips were curled in a fierce snarl.

Chapter
Twenty

Will left the dun to fend for itself, racing through the sotol in a crouch while shedding his duster. He dropped the coat behind him and made for cover, gripping his rifle in one hand and the .44 in the other, fully expecting the roar of a gun. Moving away from the spot where Iron Horse sighted him had come as a reflex, an instinct for survival. When he stumbled to a halt behind a clump of thicker sotol, the silence of the Comanche's rifle puzzled him.

A horse nickered near the spring, then the patter of hooves rose in the still morning air. Will's gelding answered the mustang pony with a whicker of its own, marking the place where it was hidden in the brush. Will gasped for breath, unwilling to rise above the leaves for a look toward the rock. Did the hoofbeats mean that Iron Horse was riding away from the spring? Will waited without breathing, seeking to identify the direction the galloping horse was taking. Were the sounds growing louder? Or were his ears playing tricks on him?

He was sure his aching lungs would burst before he could judge where the running pony was headed, thus he sought a quick mouthful of air. Turning his head slightly changed the sounds, and now he was sure the hoofbeats came from a single horse. Had the girl broken free of her captor? Or was Iron Horse charging toward Will on the back of the pinto in a show of Comanche courage? There was no doubt now— the racing hooves were moving toward him. The thump of pounding hoofbeats was growing louder.

Will's thumb pulled back the hammer of his Walker. The

approaching pony galloped faster. Every muscle in his body tensed for action. He clamped his teeth together, eyes darting back and forth across the irregular shapes of the plants around him. Seconds stretched to an eternity while he waited for the first glimpse of a red and white pinto coat among the sotol stalks.

Suddenly the hoofbeats changed direction, requiring only an instant for Will to guess what purpose lay behind it. Now the sounds moved toward the spot where he'd left his dun ground-hitched. "The son of a bitch!" Will growled.

He took off in a lumbering run for his horse just as a splash of color appeared between the spiny leaves. The pinto pony charged through the plants, ears flattened against its neck, its tail streaming behind. The pony's head bobbed up and down with the power of its run. Will scrambled over uncertain footing, aiming his .44 at a spot just above the pinto's withers where a rider should have been. Finger curled around the pistol's trigger, Will ran faster, for he knew why he couldn't see Iron Horse. The Indian was hanging off the side of his speeding calico mount. The daring Comanche maneuver was an illusion, making the horse appear riderless. Will Dobbs had been fooled by the trick a long time ago, but not now. Fort Mason's bitter lessons were carved into his soul. He dropped the .44's sights only slightly and squeezed the trigger.

The bark of the gun made Will's stride falter, then he caught himself and kept running. The pinto's knees buckled and it went down heavily, sprawling on its chest among the sotol trunks. Dust boiled from the ground where the animal collapsed. Will heard a grunt above the rhythmic thumping of his boots; he thumbed back the hammer again and rushed toward the downed pony as fast as his feet would carry him. The yellow dust swirled and began to settle, still preventing him from seeing the Indian, though he knew Iron Horse was there—somewhere in the veil of airborne caliche powder. The Comanche might be stunned by the fall, but the Indian would come up fighting unless he got to him first.

Will raced up to the heels of the crumpled mustang much

too quickly, before the dust had cleared, in his haste to kill the Indian. Just as he skidded to a halt near the pony carcass, a darker shape arose behind the filmy curtain of settling chalk. He swung the muzzle of his gun too late. A hammerlike blow struck his wrist, knocking the .44 from his grasp. The Walker exploded as it arced above Will's head, then a hand seized the barrel of his Winchester, wresting it from his fingers before his grip tightened.

Will dove blindly at the Indian's chest, commanding all the spring his legs could muster. He felt his body slam against rock-hard muscles that would not yield, and the force of the collision drove all the air from his lungs with a deep grunt of surprise and pain. Will's fingers clawed for anything he could grasp. His right hand closed around the soft flesh of the Comanche's throat in a stroke of sheer blind luck. Suddenly Will found himself staring into a pair of obsidian eyes slitted with hatred.

A chilling scream burst from the throat of Iron Horse as the two foes struggled for any advantage. Feet churned for a purchase while Will's left hand sought the arm that wrenched away his rifle. Something crashed into Will's right ear, bringing flashing pinpoints of light to his eyes. He felt his knees sag, then the muscular Indian swung him to the ground, landing hard atop his chest when his fingers would not release their viselike grip from around the Comanche's windpipe.

Their eyes met again, faces only inches apart, sinewy arms battling each other's strength, legs and feet thrashing for leverage on sunbaked soil. Will's free hand found the Comanche's thick wrist and closed around it. Muscles bunched in the Indian's chest, and Will felt the renegade's incredible power drive him back to the ground. Ropy cords of muscle stood out in Iron Horse's neck, loosening Will's fingers away from the windpipe for a ragged intake of whistling air. Locked in a deadly embrace with the Comanche, Will knew he stood no chance of overpowering him hand to hand. Staring into the hard black eyes hovering over him, he understood the nature of his enemy now. Iron Horse was part man, part animal. His animal instincts governed how the fight would be waged. He would kill his adversary any way he could. There would be no rules.

Will's arms began to tremble violently under the Comanche's weight. Iron Horse felt his advantage and shifted his body for a thrust downward. Suddenly Will's right leg was free. Summoning all his strength, he jerked his knee up as quickly as he could into the soft bulge of the Indian's testicles. Iron Horse catapulted over Will's head, grimacing, though he made no sound, no cry of pain.

Will rolled to his left, scrambling to his knees, then he sprang upon the Comanche's back. Iron Horse whirled despite the crush of Will's body, swinging an elbow into Will's cheek. Will fought to stay on top of the Indian, tasting blood from the smashing blow across his face. The rifle had landed beside Iron Horse when he fell, but there was no time to make a grab for it when split seconds counted. Will swung a fist downward with all his might. Knuckles cracked against the Comanche's skull. He felt Iron Horse stiffen between his legs. White-hot pain shot up Will's arm.

Iron Horse roared, arching his spine, clawing for Will's face with thick, curled fingers. Will aimed a looping punch and struck the Indian's nose. Cartilage snapped and warm blood squirted up Will's forearm. Clawing fingernails scraped across Will's face and eyes. Searing pain followed the fingers down to Will's throat, then a grip like iron enclosed his neck and the body underneath him bucked suddenly, lunging off the ground.

Will sucked in a strangled breath. His throat was being crushed, and now time was even more precious. The Comanche's grip would soon render him unconscious. He steadied himself on the Indian's chest and rode the powerful surge until Iron Horse fell back to the caliche. Will's vision started to blur, shut off from his supply of air. His next move was critical—the fingers had to be driven away from his throat before he blacked out.

His hand found the wrist beneath his chin and slid up to the thumb, buried deep in the flesh of his neck. He dug two fingers into his own skin and curled them around the thumb.

Blood poured into Will's eyes and filled his mouth. He threw all his strength into a downward pull toward the wrist. Bone cracked. He sucked air and blood into his lungs when he heard the sound, then his vision slowly cleared of flashing lights.

Iron Horse writhed underneath him, lips drawn back to show teeth stained by the blood running from his broken nose. Will sent a ball of knuckles toward the face and felt the shock all the way to his shoulder. Muscles went slack in the Comanche's arms and legs when the blow thudded into his temple. It was all the time Will needed to make a dive for the rifle, free at last of the steely grip around his neck.

He landed flat and seized the Winchester with slippery fingers, gasping, fighting a reeling dizziness washing through his skull as he whirled over on his back to level the gun. Iron Horse had come to a crouch, coiling for a lunge, when the muzzle of the rifle swung toward his chest. The Indian hesitated just long enough for Will to cock the hammer. Iron Horse leapt forward. In the same instant, Will's trigger finger curled.

The explosion thundered across the mesa, echoing from the sotol around the two men. Iron Horse floated trough the air toward the gun, then his torso jerked in mid-flight. A spout of crimson shot skyward from the hole in his back when the piece of molten lead passed through him.

The big Comanche fell slowly back to earth and landed facedown with a muffled thump, arms and legs askew. Will blinked and inched backward, not quite trusting his eyes until he sleeved away the blood trickling down his face. With the gunshot still ringing in his ears, he scrambled to his knees while working the lever of the Winchester. The spent shell clattered to the ground, then there was silence.

Will's sides were heaving. Fresh pain awakened in his broken knuckles and in the torn flesh of his neck. The scratches across his face prickled with a thousand fiery needles, but he was alive, and that single thought muted the pains. He stared at the body of Iron Horse, a mere three feet away, knowing it was a measurement of how close he had come to dying. His life had been saved by a gun, as it had been more times than he cared to count. Without the Winchester he held in trembling, blood-reddened hands, the victory would have belonged to Iron Horse.

When he was sure of the Indian's death, he struggled to his feet with the aid of the rifle stock. Air had never tasted so sweet as it did now. He spent a minute swaying on uncertain legs, trying to regain his full senses, savoring each breath until his mind was clear. When his breathing slowed, he took stock of things around him. The dead pinto lay where it had fallen, and the sight sickened him. It had been necessary to drop the pony, though now he grieved for the beautiful animal as a man who loved good horses. To the east his dun wandered among the sotols searching for grass. Only then did he remember Osate, turning his gaze toward the spring.

His feet obeyed his commands reluctantly when he started for the rock, his brain still slightly awash with dizzy sickness. Feeling returned to most of his body, making him aware of a damp sensation around his right shoulder. He continued toward the spring in a slow, stumbling walk, his rifle balanced in one hand, reaching for the dampness with the other. When he drew his fingertips from his shirt, he saw blood. He remembered that he'd lost his hat and pistol in the fight as he touched a sore spot above his ear. He felt a tear in his scalp where his hatband should have been, and knew it was the source of the bleeding. Only vaguely, he had a recollection of the blow to his head during the struggle. Blood trickled down his face from the scratches, and he forced a dry laugh, figuring he looked more like the loser of the battle than a winner just then. When he looked down, his pale blue shirt was a dirty red.

He approached the slab of limestone on leaden legs, searching for the cavern Pablo described. Starting around the rock, he merely glanced at the brown mare, too concerned about Osate for the moment to think about horses. His boots crunched across loose rock as he began his circle around to the far side of the slab. A few steps more and he saw a dark opening below a lip of the boulder.

He crouched at the entrance and peered inside. "Osate!" he shouted hoarsely.

"Cap-en," a voice cried from somewhere in the depths of the cave.

A slow smile lifted the ends of his handlebar mustache. He entered the hole and crept forward, smelling damp smells. Until his eyes adjusted to the dark, he felt his way along the cavern wall. Then he saw the faint reflection of light from the entrance on a pool of water, and beside it the huddled form of the girl, her hands and feet bound together.

"Cap-en," she said softly when he knelt beside her.

He placed the rifle next to him and started to untie a strip of leather binding her wrists. "It's okay now," he whispered, noticing that his dizziness had suddenly grown worse. "Iron Horse is dead," he added in a phlegmy voice, steadying himself on his knees.

The moment the girl's hands were free, she reached for his face, touching one of the scratches. He started to tell her how the scratches got there, preparing the words he would say, when the light from the mouth of the cave dimmed. He felt himself falling very slowly to one side, and could do nothing to halt his fall toward a velvety blanket of unconsciousness.

Hazy images came and went. Something cool passed across his face. His eyelids felt so heavy that no amount of effort could hold them open at first. Then gradually he awakened to find himself resting against the rock at the mouth of the cavern.

He stirred, glancing around, aware that his shirt was gone. He sat bare-chested in warm sunlight. His dun gelding and the brown mare stood to one side of the slab, their reins tethered to a sotol stump. Then he heard movement in the cave, and saw Osate emerge into the light with a piece of damp cloth.

She smiled and came over to him. His gaze drifted down, for it was then that he noticed she was naked. The shirt he'd given her was balled in her hands, dribbling water. She took a part of the cloth and wiped it gently over his face and the gash above his ear. Her bare breasts rocked with the motion of her arm. He simply stared at them until his eyes went to her pretty face, where they remained.

"You sleep long, Cap-en," she said, fixing him with a lingering look.

"You're a beautiful woman," he said thickly, all else forgotten.

"What is . . . beautiful?" she asked.

He wondered how to explain. "Nice to look at. Pretty."

Her puzzled expression proved his failure at the attempt. How could he make her understand? When it was clear that words would not work, he lifted his arms and slowly placed his palms on either side of her face. Leaning away from the rock, he kissed her lightly on the lips, half expecting her to pull away. But she remained on her knees beside him and did not retreat from the gentle pressure of his mouth.

"Like that," he said, grinning. "That's what a man does when a woman is beautiful."

"Funny . . . touch," she answered, lips parting in a smile. Then she bent closer and opened her mouth to be kissed again, slowly closing her dark brown eyes.

When he placed his lips over hers, she made a soft purring sound and pressed against his chest, flattening her breasts onto his bare skin. A tingle of excitement ran down Will's arms as he wrapped them around her tiny waist. Osate's body shuddered with pleasure. A low moan whispered up her neck while her fingers worked into the long curls of his unshorn hair. Very slowly she lifted a shapely leg to straddle him, then she settled across his lap. He allowed his hands to slide down to the soft flesh of her hips, where he cupped his palms. The girl shivered in his grasp and moaned again, opening her mouth wider, kissing him harder. He could hear Osate's breath coming faster. Her breasts rose and fell against his ribs. For now, he was lost in the pleasure of her nearness. The duel to the death with Iron Horse was forgotten while he embraced the beautiful Lipan woman.

Chapter
Twenty-one

He stood beside Osate in purpling twilight, gazing down at the body of Iron Horse. Even in death there was something sinister about the giant Comanche that made Will uneasy. If he needed more proof of the Indian's cruelty, it was the shriveled bullet pouch dangling from the renegade's horsehair belt, fashioned from a woman's breast. And there was more, the brittle scalp locks tied to the stock and muzzle of the Winchester rifle lying beside the pinto stallion. Gentler folk found it hard to believe stories about Comanche savagery, but the few who who survived Comanche attacks knew the truth firsthand. No other race practiced this kind of butchery. Their fearsome reputation was justly deserved.

Will turned for his horse. The slaughter of innocent settlers at Lajitas had been avenged, and he meant to put this assignment behind him as quickly as he could. There was still the matter of Diente Oro to be handled, though he doubted the Comancheros would venture north of the border again. He pulled himself wearily over his saddle and looked south over dusk-darkened land. This part of Texas would be peaceful for a while. The Comanche problem had been put to rest.

Osate climbed aboard her mare, and when Will looked at her, his mood softened. The girl was a lone bright spot in an otherwise grisly affair. He'd been lucky to save her from the clutches of Iron Horse. It was something his conscience demanded—that he make the attempt alone the way he did, without risking the lives of his men. After what had happened

to Tasa, he felt he owed the girl something for the help the
Lipans gave the Rangers.

He swung the dun and moved off among the sotol shadows, thankful to be alive as they rode to the edge of the mesa
to begin the descent. His scalp wound throbbed and the
scratches on his face were a nuisance when they stung him
now and then, but all in all he would make no complaint.
Not many men outlived a hand-to-hand encounter with a
Comanche. Lady Luck had shown him one of her rare smiles.

While the gelding picked its way down the slope, he wondered about the fate of his men. If their luck held, Billy and
the others would find the Comanchero camp empty.

Osate trotted her mare up beside him when they reached
level ground. The night would turn cool and she would be
cold, clad only in the shirt, thus Will shouldered out of his
coat and leaned out of the saddle to offer it to her. She took
the duster and was briefly troubled putting on unfamiliar
white man's attire. They'd eaten some of the goat meat while
Will's clothing dried in the sun. Now that he was rested, he
meant to ride most of the night until they found the other
Rangers, likely just after dawn.

Turning south, they entered a meandering dry wash at a
jog trot that would be easy on the horses. Above them stars
sprinkled ebony skies. They rode side by side in silence,
listening to the iron-shod hooves.

Shafts of golden sunshine slanted into the basin. Sparrows
chirped from cottonwood branches around the spring. A doe
lifted its muzzle on the far side of the pool, dribbling water
onto the glassy surface, making a sound like soft chimes.
The deer flagged its tail, then stamped a forefoot in the mud
at the water's edge. A wary buck moved in deeper shadows
inside the cottonwood grove, preparing for flight at the doe's
warning signal. Somewhere in the treetops a bluejay uttered
its shrill, harsh call. Fluttering wings moved higher in the
branches to be away from the danger.

Santiago Cortez rolled to his haunches, peering to the north
from his wooden prison, alerted by the actions of the birds

and deer. He cocked his head to listen. His stomach grumbled with desperate hunger now, and the noise prevented him
from hearing distant sounds. For days he'd eaten almost nothing in an attempt to save what little dried beef he had left,
and sipped sparingly from the bucket so he wouldn't die of
thirst until someone came. He had practiced breathing
through his mouth so he wouldn't notice the ripe smell in the
cage. But there was no escape from the swarms of black flies.
No matter what he did, they clung to his skin. Batting them
away from his face only made him tired, and once, he'd
driven one into his mouth. While he dozed in the shade, flies
entered his nostrils and sat on his lips, awakening him so
often they'd almost driven him mad.

Santiago straightened and stepped over to bars of mesquite
for a better look, avoiding piles of excrement until he stood
with his hands wrapped around two of the stakes, one eye
pressed to an opening. At times he'd tried to kick through
the walls where he suspected there might be a weak place,
but the rawhide bindings held fast. The bars roofing the cage
could not be budged either, and at last he'd given up in frus-
tration and exhaustion, knowing he must save his strength if
he meant to outlive his meager food supply. Or his water.

The northern entrance into the basin was empty, and he
wondered what had frightened the deer. For a time he stood
with his face to the bars, listening. Were the Rangers coming
back? *"Bastardos,"* he whispered, remembering the four
white men. Iron Horse would kill them all, torturing them if
he could. But then who would come to save him from star-
vation? Why had Diente Oro not returned? Could it be that
el jefe was afraid of the four Rangers? Was this possible?

Santiago feared only one of them, the heavy Tejano who
held the shotgun below his chin. That one was *un idiota*, he
remembered. If it had not been for the tall one wearing the
mustache, the *capitán*, he was certain he would have died
that day. The big Tejano wanted to kill him. Hadn't he begged
the *capitán* to let him shoot off his head? *Dios!*

Nothing moved in the passageway. Santiago's heart sank
and he wheeled away from the bars. A fly buzzed near his

ear as he made his way carefully to the water bucket. He kept the last strip of jerky in a pocket of his vest to keep it from the flies. Today he would have to eat some of it, maybe only half. Never before had he been so hungry, making his legs weak and his head spin. Never in all his life could he imagine being kept in a cage like this, to die slowly.

Leaves rustled suddenly in the cottonwoods. Sparrows darted away from the trees. The buck and the doe bounded out of the grove, fleeing south. Santiago knew something had startled the animals. He froze against the wall of the cage, squinting northward. What had frightened the deer and the birds? What was out there? He saw nothing in the passageway or high on the rim.

Silence blanketed the basin, heavy, thick. Santiago's heart made a thumping sound. Who was coming? What had driven the wild creatures from the spring? His heart beat faster.

A sharp whistle resounded from the top of the canyon, and when he heard it, Santiago smiled. He placed two fingers in his mouth and blew an answer to the hawk's call. Diente Oro had not forgotten his faithful servant after all. He had come back to free him from this stinking cage. *El jefe* was not afraid of the Tejanos.

Excitement filled Santiago's chest. He hurried to the gate of his prison and gave the padlock a one-sided leer. "Diente Oro will chew this chain in half with his teeth!" he promised. "Then we will go looking for the cowardly Tejanos who did this to me! We will make them pay for taking the lives of poor Alfred and the others!"

He could barely contain himself, thinking of revenge, waiting for *el jefe* to come for him and open the gate. With a look of disdain at the water bucket, he swung a boot and kicked it over, paying no heed to the scant contents dampening the pale earth near his feet. Santiago began making plans to kill a deer as soon as he was released. He would eat the entire hindquarter himself, the delicious backstrap first, perhaps seasoned with chilis. His mouth watered, planning how he would gorge himself with succulent deer meat. His terrible hunger would be put to rest. He seized the gate in both hands and shook it violently, rattling the chain and lock. In minutes he would be a free man.

He heard horses coming from the north. His hands relaxed on the gate to watch Diente Oro ride into the basin. Bushy eyebrows knitted on his forehead when he saw the riders swing around a turn in the passage. There was something about the men, but what was it? What was making them look different? Was it only the distance?

Then he knew the cause of his concern, when he focused on the hats the men wore. The riders were Tejanos, not his *compadres* in sombreros.

"Rangers!" he hissed, balling his hands into angry fists. Three Tejanos rode slowly into the basin, leading a fourth riderless horse. Perhaps one of the Rangers had been killed by Iron Horse, maybe the *idiota*?

Santiago despaired over his poor fortunes, yet some indefinable thing still puzzled him about the Tejanos' return. Why had he been so certain of his release moments before?

The signal! Suddenly he remembered the night hawk's whistle from the rim. It was a signal known only to Diente Oro's pistoleros and the *Indios*.

Santiago's beard widened in a wicked grin. He gazed up at the top of the canyon, but only briefly, so he would not give Diente Oro away. The *estupido* Tejanos were riding into *el jefe*'s ambush. In seconds guns would start blazing from the rim and the Rangers would be cut down.

He found the big Tejano among the three and focused on him to wait for the killing to begin. Santiago wanted to watch the tough-talking *bastardo* fall from his horse when the shooting started. It would please him greatly to see the Ranger die.

Thinking about the moment when bullets came flying from every direction, Santiago crept backward and settled on his haunches against the wall of the cage. He still grinned in anticipation. Diento Oro had been very wise to wait for the Tejanos return. Now he could kill them all. "I only wish *el jefe* had brought me something to eat," he said under his breath. "The waiting would have been easier. . . ."

A gun roared from the lip of the basin, broadening Santiago's grin. Then rifles crackled almost in unison around the canyon rim. The Rangers' horses bolted and men began to fall from their saddles amid the withering gunfire from above.

He watched the big Ranger fall heavily in a cloud of dust, and the sight made Santiago feel like cheering. But when he looked closer at the spot where the Tejano fell, he saw nothing but dirt. One of the men was running in a crouch toward an adobe near the empty corrals. Another dodged back and forth through the dust from the horses' heels until Santiago lost sight of him in a tangle of mesquites. It didn't seem possible that two of the Rangers survived the hail of bullets, And what of the big *idiota*? Where was he?

Heavy-bore rifles started to bang from the basin floor. Lead whined through the air. A slug ricocheted off the adobe behind Santiago and its deadly song sent him sprawling on his face in drying offal. The thud of rifles danced back and forth from the Rangers' hiding places. Answering fire poured down from above. Flies swarmed around Santiago's head and he tasted something bitter clinging to his lips, but he would not risk lifting his head when so many bullets were flying over him. A chunk of lead splintered a bar of his cage. The sound made him shiver.

A short pause in the shooting permitted Santiago to raise his face slightly, for he heard running feet close by. Spur rowels banged toward him—one of the Tejanos was coming. Was it the one he feared? Was he coming to keep his promise to shoot off his head?

More gunfire erupted near the corrals, and again the sing-song of speeding lead followed the explosions. Santiago buried his face in his hands and wept silently, shuddering, wondering if this was to be his last moment on earth, wondering if he would feel pain when the Tejano's huge shotgun swept away his skull. Between sobs he began mouthing words from a prayer he remembered from his childhood while he fingered the beads of his mother's rosary.

Pounding guns sounded all around him. He kept his eyes tightly closed and tried to recall every word of the prayer.

Chapter
Twenty-two

Billy silently cursed his carelessness, blaming it on his fever. It was his fault that they found themselves in this fix. He'd led the company into the jaws of a trap like some damn greenhorn. Now they were pinned down by an unknown number of riflemen, with no way to escape from the basin. Carl had taken a bullet in the shoulder during the first fusillade from above. It was unbelievable good luck that none of them had been killed when the shooting started. The fever made Billy light-headed. All night he'd been shivering inside his thin coat like a newborn calf in a snowstorm. This morning, he'd been half asleep.

Gunfire came from all sides, preventing Billy from leaving the doorway of the adobe. Spent slugs plowed tiny furrows in the dirt beyond the opening. Occasional balls of lead flattened against the walls of dried mud, spewing gritty particles. The Rangers' ammunition was in their saddlebags, and now their frightened horses milled about the basin. Making the try to reach the boxes of shells would be outright suicide. Gold Tooth Valdez had been awaiting his chance for revenge, and Billy Blue handed it to him on a silver platter.

He'd only had a brief glimpse of Leon when the first volley sent everyone diving from their saddles. Billy had been too startled by the surprise attack to do much more than seek shelter from the hail of lead. Leon was somewhere in the trees, firing now and then before changing positions. Carl was inside another adobe, shooting less often, making Billy wonder how serious his shoulder wound might be. It would be inviting death to make a run for the hut where Carl was hiding, but someone had to help him. The task fell to him, Billy knew, since Will had left him in charge when he went looking for Iron Horse and the woman.

"You've gone an' done it now, Billy boy," he told himself, eyeing the distance he would run to reach Carl. "You put everybody's neck in a noose this time."

A lone gunshot cracked from high atop the canyon, giving off a spit of white smoke. Billy raised his rifle to his shoulder and drew a bead just in back of the spot, ignoring the sudden chatter of more guns around him. Peering along the Winchester barrel, he waited for something to move near the basin rim where the shot had come from. As a man who hunted for bounty, he'd learned the value of patience. He held his breath, paying no attention to the battle sounds. If a well-placed shot took just one Comanchero out of the fight, his time was not wasted.

A smudge of dark color appeared above the ledge. Billy raised his sights to allow for the distance and feathered the trigger with a soft stroke of his finger. The Winchester jumped in his hands, driving the butt plate into his shoulder when gunpowder ignited with a roar. Swollen skin around his wound prickled with pain as the kick of the gun bent him backward, yet he kept his eye on the slight movement he'd seen on the ledge. Instantly the object stirred again when the bullet found its mark. The head and chest of a man arose from the shelter of a rock pile, then tilted forward, over the edge. Billy watched the body slip off the rim and tumble down, spiraling as it fell, arms clawing empty air. Billy turned his head just before the gunman landed. A drop of hundreds of feet made it unnecessary to be sure of the final result.

A rifle blasted from the cottonwoods around the spring, two shots in quick succession. Lead whined off the face of the canyon wall. A distant gun answered Leon's volley. Bullets pattered into the trees. A branch swayed, tossing leaves about, making a soft rustling until the limb stilled. Now there was a pause in the shooting, as though someone had commanded everyone to hold their fire.

A sound caught Billy's attention. Horses were trotting out

of the basin, bringing a sinking feeling to the pit of his stomach. The ammunition was out of reach on the backs of their horses. The Rangers would be counting bullets now, making every shot count, until the last shell was used. Pinned down on the basin floor as they were, there was no chance of making an escape. It was only a matter of time before the Rangers' guns were empty. Then Valdez would send his men down to begin the executions.

"Wish the hell Will would show up," he said quietly, though he knew there was a darker possibility. Will Dobb's scalp might be decorating the belt around Iron Horse's belly right about now. Will could have gotten careless once too often, the way he himself had this morning.

The lull in the shooting continued, and the quiet permitted time for him to think. He couldn't wait for the off chance that Captain Dobbs would arrive to untangle the mess they were in. He had to do something, and whatever he did, it needed to be done damn quick or they'd be fighting the Comancheros with empty guns. He glanced across the barren hardpan to the adobe where Carl was hidden. The first order of business was to see to Carl's shoulder.

The silence lengthened. Billy fingered his rifle, judging the distance he had to run. "Now's as good a time as any," he told himself. A fever chill made him tremble briefly. Or was it the product of fear, knowing the chance he was about to take?

He came to the edge of the door frame, took a deep breath, then raced away from the hut in a zigzag crouch. Ten yards away from the adobe a gun popped at the top of the canyon. Swerving hard to the right, he heard the bullet richochet off the wall behind him. Then a staccato of gunfire sounded from all sides, drowning out the pounding of his boots across the caliche. Fresh pain awakened in his side and still he kept running, dodging back and forth to make a poor target. Tiny puffs of dust spitted from the ground around his feet as whistling lead followed his pathway toward Carl. He stumbled once and almost fell flat on his face, yet some inner reserve of energy drove him onward at a dangerous forward tilt. Now

so many rifles were firing at him from above that he was sure
he'd never make the last twenty yards to safety. Throwing
caution to the wind at a time like this looked certain to cost
him his life. In a final surge of desperate effort, he abandoned
all hope of dodging slugs and ran straight for the door of the
hut. A speeding ball of lead tore off his hat. A breath of fast-
moving air brushed his cheek just as he made a dive for the
entrance. Something splattered above his head while he was
airborne, then he crashed into the adobe wall beyond the
doorway, landing shoulder first and crumpling to the floor,
groaning as he fell.

Bullets skittered into the dark room and bounced dully on
the ground around him, deflected by the dirt wall above his
head. A stab of blinding pain coursed from his shoulder while
he scrambled away from the opening in a belly-crawl. He
was panting and didn't hear what Carl was saying to him
when a hand grabbed his coat collar to pull him from the line
of fire.

"What?" he gasped, trying to focus on Carl's face in the
half light, struggling to his feet.

"I said that took guts, Billy," Carl replied, helping Billy
steady himself, "but you shoulda stayed where you was."

Billy saw a dark bloodstain on the right sleeve of Carl's
duster. "I knew you were hit," he said, between wheezing
breaths. "Came over . . . to see what I could do."

"Hell, it ain't nothin'," Carl spat, turning to glare out a
window angrily. "Hardly a scratch. You risked your hide fer
nothin', partner. They damn near cut you down out
there. . . ."

Billy took a moment to collect himself. "Had to do somethin'. We can't just sit here till we're out of ammunition.
Soon as I catch my wind, I'm gonna try to figure a way to
climb outta here. One of us has gotta get behind 'em up
yonder."

Carl nodded. "I'd go, if it wasn't for this goddamn sore
arm," he said savagely. 'I'd like nothin' better'n the chance
to sneak up behind the bastards."

"I can do it, if there's a way to the top," Billy said, moving over to the window for a look outside. "First off, we'll see to that hole in your shoulder. There's a good-sized stand of mesquites out in back of this hut. If I can get out this door without catchin' a slug, I can work my way around without drawin' so much fire.''

The rattling guns fell silent, and the quiet seemed strange after the crescendo of noise that followed Billy to the adobe. For a time Billy studied the lay of things. "Pull off that coat,'' he said absently, without taking his eyes from the scene outside the window. "Let's see how bad it is. . . .''

"I done told you it's just a scratch,'' Carl grumbled, leaning his Winchester against the wall, then sliding the shoulder strap on the Greener down his good arm.

When Billy looked at Carl, he saw the big Ranger wince, tracing a finger over the tear in his shirt where the bullet went through.

"Worse'n you thought, ain't it?'' Billy asked.

"Too far from my heart to kill me,'' he answered, tight-voiced, pain written plainly on his face.

Billy came over to inspect the wound. Torn muscle lay below a flap of bloody skin. "That slug's gotta come out,'' he said softly, knowing how much pain Carl would have to endure when a heated knife blade followed the bullet's trajectory to dig it out. "It'll have to wait . . .'bout all I can do now is stop the bleeding.''

"Sure as hell wish I had some whiskey,'' Carl whispered.

Billy opened his shirt to remove a strip of the bandage he wore over his stitches. "We make a hell of a pair, don't we?'' he asked, working his mouth to a weak grin. "Both of us got more holes in our hides than any feller needs.''

The bandage stemmed the blood flow. As soon as the cloth was knotted, Billy crept back to the window. Not a shot had been fired while he attended to Carl's injury, though he wondered just how long the silence would last.

Beyond the adobe lay the grisly remains of the Comancheros Leon had assembled after the first encounter with Valdez. Some of the corpses were bloated. Others had been torn apart by hungry coyotes and wolves. In one of the stockades,

Santiago Cortez huddled in a corner. The sun had climbed higher, warming the basin. A gentle breeze moved through the trees, stirring late autumn leaves here and there. If he hadn't known about the riflemen encircling the canyon, it would have seemed a peaceful scene.

"Wonder where Leon is?" he asked, sweeping a look around the basin floor without sighting the Ranger. "Before I make a try at getting to the top, I oughta tell him what I aim to do."

Carl edged up to the far side of the window, cradling his rifle in the crook of his good arm. "Maybe he's gone up there himself," Carl suggested. "He'll be mad about the way these Meskins tried to gun us down. He'll be lookin' fer a way to kill 'em."

"He won't remember that the cap'n told us to take prisoners," Billy remarked wryly. "Soon as that first shot was fired, he forgot what the cap'n said."

Carl grunted. "Makes it worse when it's Meskins he's after. His brain don't work at all whilst he's tryin' to kill Meskins."

Wind gusted around the spring, swaying treetops. A few yellow leaves fell slowly from moving branches to the earth, some becoming golden dervishes as they whirled downward. Billy couldn't find Leon among the cottonwood trunks. "I hope he didn't go up there on his own," he said thoughtfully, puzzling over Leon's absence. "Until I know where he is, I'd better wait here. . . ."

Noonday sun shone down on the basin floor. The waiting was getting on Billy's nerves. Leon was nowhere to be found. No shots had been fired, and now the quiet had grown eerie. Billy knew it was too quiet. Something was afoot up on the rim, some event that kept the Comancheros from shooting. But what was it? Why hadn't Valdez ordered his men to keep the Rangers wary of making a break by firing once in a while? The hours of silence made no sense. What the hell was going on up there?

"Wonder if ol' Leon got shot down someplace?" Carl

asked in a hoarse voice. "Maybe he's . . . dead? Can't figure why we ain't seen him no place."

Billy sighed, chewing his lip absently, more worried now than ever. "I can't explain it either. Looks like he'd show himself once in a while, so we'd know he's alive."

Carl offered no further opinions and neither did Billy. Billy didn't want to think about the prospects of Leon's death. They'd known each other too many years for Billy to consider it. Another slow hour passed while the two Rangers watched the basin from the window.

"I never was much for drinkin' whiskey," Billy said later, "but I'd take a drink or two right about now, to settle my nerves. This waitin' is making me edgy as hell. Hard to figure why it's so damn quiet."

"Wish you wouldn't talk about needin' a drink," Carl complained. "I'd fight a grizzly bear with a willow switch fer just one good drink of sour mash."

Billy aimed a look north, simply passing time, letting his eyes drift to the mouth of the passageway where they'd ridden in this morning. He stiffened suddenly when he saw shapes moving, and in the same instant his hand clawed for his rifle.

"Look yonder!" he cried, swinging the Winchester to his shoulder in a lightning-fast arc. "They're comin', Carl! Get ready!"

Carl scrambled to the door frame with his rifle, peering northward. A man was walking brazenly around a bend in the passage, then another appeared behind the first.

"What the hell. . . ?" Billy's question died on his lips when he saw a third man join the procession. The three seemed to be marching in a vaguely military fashion into the basin.

"Maybe they've gone loco in this heat," Carl surmised. "They act like gents leadin' a damn parade. Hell, looks like they're askin' us to blow their heads off. They're comin' in range. . . ."

"Hold off a minute," Billy said, tipping the muzzle of the Winchester, frowning. "Somethin' don't add up."

Both men watched the three Comancheros approach the

huts. One Mexican cast a curious shadow. Billy noticed that they were not carrying rifles, no weapons of any kind. The big Comanchero marching at the rear appeared to be moving more stiffly than the others. For the moment, Billy was too astonished for words. Fifty yards more and the men would be in range of their Winchesters.

Now he saw what made the last Mexican walk differently, and the explanation for his odd-shaped shadow. Parading right behind the heavyset man, Leon Graves followed closely. Leon's skinny frame had been hidden from Billy and Carl. Sunlight glittered on the barrel of the pistol Leon held against the Mexican's skull and off the rifle dangling beside his left leg. Leon marched the line of men toward the adobe where Billy and Carl stood dumbfounded at the windowsill.

"I'll be damned," Carl breathed, lowering his Winchester. "Ol' Leon got 'em all by hisself. Yonder's a miracle, Billy. There's three live Meskins when Leon's carryin' a gun."

"It's plumb amazin'," Billy agreed. "The cap'n ain't never gonna believe it when we tell him how it happened. He'll call us both liars when he hears about it." Billy swung away from the window. "We'd best hurry out there afore Leon changes his mind." He started to the doorway, squinting when bright light hit his eyes. "That's three mighty lucky Mexicans," he added softly, afraid to completely trust Leon's apparent benevolence.

Carl followed Billy outside. They turned from the hut and went toward Leon and his prisoners. Carl carried his bad shoulder low, walking gingerly alongside Billy. Just once Billy glanced up at the top of the canyon, trying to guess how Leon got up there unnoticed by the Comancheros and how he got the drop on them.

Will Dobbs would never believe it. Never in a million years.

"How'd you do it?" Billy asked. The three Mexicans were safely in the wooden cage with Santiago Cortez after Carl shattered the padlock with the Greener.

Leon hooked his thumbs in his gun belt. He'd been staring at Gold Tooth Valdez until Billy's question distracted him. "What you done was a big help," he began. "You drew their fire when you made that run over to Carl. Saw my chance, an' I took it. There's a footpath over yonder that leads to the top. Come to a place or two where it was hard to climb, but I made it. I reckon it's where they sent somebody up to post a lookout." Then Leon's gaze fell back on Valdez. "First hombre I run across was ol' Gold Tooth himself. Lyin' up in a bunch of rocks. When I stuck my gun next to his cheek and swore I'd blow him another hole he could spit through, he went plumb pale an' dropped his gun. Sure was wishin' he'd try me, but the yellow sumbitch came quiet as a kitten. Before I brung him an' the others down, I thought about knockin' out that shiny tooth with the butt of my six-gun, so I'd have me a keepsake. Then I remembered what Cap'n Dobbs said about takin' prisoners so the gov'nor can hang 'em. This here gent will be a whole lot prettier when he gets his neck stretched if he's got that tooth in his mouth. Soon as he starts to choke, folks will see it. Gonna be a mighty pretty sight when the sun shines on that hunk o' gold. Gov'nor Davis will be real pleased."

Valdez glared at Leon. Heavy muscles knotted in his chest as he tested the iron manacles binding his wrists together. When he spoke, the gold in his mouth gleamed. "You are a coward, gringo!"

Carl answered the Comanchero before Leon could form a reply to the insult. "You're too dumb to know how lucky you are," Carl spat, leaning closer to the bars. "This here Ranger you called a coward ain't never forgot about the Alamo. Take a look over yonder at that pile of dead Meskins. Leon killed damn near all of 'em, the ones I didn't shoot. He'd have killed you the same, if the cap'n hadn't asked fer somebody the governor could hang." A snarl drew Carl's lips across his teeth. "I'm gonna enjoy watchin' you dance a jig at the end of a rope. Soon as your feet start kickin', I'm gonna bust out laughin' real loud. It'll be the last sound you

ever hear, me an' Leon havin' a good laugh while you
choke!''

Billy turned away from the cage, weary of the taunting.
He wondered what was keeping Will. Staring north, he was
forced to consider the outcome of a duel between the renegade Comanche and Will Dobbs. He counted Will among
the toughest men he had ever known, which included a size-
able handful of wanted desperadoes he'd tangled with as a
bounty hunter. But the day inevitably came when even the
toughest men found their reflexes slowed. . . .

Chapter Twenty-three

Will needed to make sure things were as they should be before he led Osate past the Comanchero camp. From the top of the basin, he saw his men lounging in the shade around the spring, and chuckled when he noticed their clothing hung up to dry on low cottonwood limbs. A bath in the pool had been too much temptation for trail-weary men. It would improve their smell after so many days in a saddle away from soap and bath water, he decided.

Beyond the cottonwoods, he could see four prisoners inside one of the mesquite stockades. "I'll be damned," he said quietly, greeted by an unexpected sight. He hadn't figured on more good luck. The capture of three more Comancheros came as additional good news.

The girl watched him closely while he mounted his horse. On the ride down, he'd tried to explain that she could not remain with him when they reached the Rio Grande. He would never be completely sure how much she understood. Several times she told him as best she could that she wanted to stay with him, using sign to add meaning when she didn't know a word. He tried to tell her that his job kept him on the move, that it wasn't possible for her to ride with him. If she understood, there was no proof of it. How could he tell her that too many things stood between them? The difference in their ages and their cultures, not to mention the nature of his profession. Down deep he knew they had been thrown together by circumstances, but now the time had come for them to return to the lives they had known before. When he thought more about it, he wondered if he could explain it to himself, much less to an Indian girl who spoke a different language. Thus he'd given up on the notion earlier in the day. He would ride with her to the Mexican border and then send her on her way to the Lipan village.

He trotted the dun away from the rim, seeking a trail to the Rio Grande before nightfall. It was better to finish the business with Osate first, before he rejoined his men.

Riding high country, he sighted the darker line of Santa Elena Canyon in the distance. Osate rode behind him in silence, rather than riding at his side as she had done before. She seemed to know what he meant to do now, and her silence was a protest.

At the river, they rode to the bank and gave the horses a drink in the shallows. Will turned to Osate and pointed across.

"You go," he said softly. "I must stay here. Go back to your people. Do you understand?"

She bowed her head. A crystal tear formed in the corner of each eye before she answered him. "Cap-en no come?" she asked.

He shook his head. "I've got a job to do," he answered, opening his duster to point to his badge. "I'm the captain of a company of Rangers. I can't go with you. And you can't stay with me."

She stared silently at the muddy current for a time, then looked at Will and heeled the mare over beside him. "I go," she whispered. Her hand came toward his face, to run a fingertip across the ends of his mustache. "Funny . . . touch," she said hoarsely, leaning off the mare's withers to kiss his mouth.

He returned the pressure of her lips, and drew back when the kiss lasted longer than he wanted. "Good-bye, Osate," he said gently, and reined his gelding out of the river. The sun was two hours from the western horizon when he urged the horse to a gallop away from the girl.

He could see the relief on Billy's face when he trotted his dun up to the spring. The bandage around Carl's shoulder distracted him when Carl trudged from the trees carrying a half-drunk bottle of plum wine. Leon's shadow moved between the trees. Only then was he satisfied, when he knew all three Rangers weren't seriously hurt.

"You're a sight for sore eyes, Cap'n," Billy said, clad only in his longjohns, as he came over to Will's horse. "You had us worried for a spell. Did you find those Injuns?"

Will came stiffly from his saddle. Every muscle in his body ached with fatigue. "I found 'em," he replied, holding on to his saddle horn for support until he knew he could trust his legs.

"Appears that pretty gal scratched the hell outta your hide," Carl observed, hobbling over to offer the bottle, amusement on his freshly shaven face.

Will sighed, remembering. "It wasn't the girl." It would be a while before he could run a razor over his cheeks; not until the cuts healed. "Had myself a run-in with Iron Horse. Got about as close to dyin' as I ever care to again."

"You kill him?" Leon asked, hurrying over just in time to hear what Will said.

"He's dead," Will answered, "but it got mighty damn close to goin' the other way." He took the bottle of wine from Carl and put it to his lips. The wine was wonderfully sweet going down his dry throat.

"Look over yonder," Leon said, pointing to the cage where the four prisoners were kept. "Saved four so's the gov'nor can hang 'em, just like you wanted. I coulda killed 'em easy, Cap'n. Sure as hell wanted to, but I done like you asked. Billy shot one off that ledge when they tried to ambush us, but we saved the rest for that noose. Ol' Gold Tooth's in with the others. Oughta make the gov'nor real proud of us when we bring these sumbitches back."

"You oughta be real proud of Leon," Carl said before Will could form a reply. "He snuck up there an' got the drop on all of 'em. He coulda blowed their heads off an' nobody'd ever knowed the difference. Leon done jus' like you told us. Sure surprised the hell outta me an' Billy."

Hearing that Leon spared the life of any men they were

after was a great surprise. The fact that all three were Mexicans left Will momentarily speechless. "I'll mention it to the major," he said when he could think. "I'll put it in my report."

Leon wore a look of pride, straightening his shoulders. "I'd like to be there to watch 'em hang," he said, "if it's all the same to the gov'nor. That way, I'll know fer sure they won't be botherin' nobody else . . . when I see 'em choke."

Will took another drink of wine and let the subject drop. He could have predicted that Leon would ask to see the hanging, given the time to follow Leon's reasoning.

"Carl's got a bullet in his shoulder," Billy said darkly, aiming a thumb at Carl's wound. "We've been lettin' him drink that wine so he won't bawl for his mother when one of us digs that slug out. I've got a knife in my saddlebags and a whet rock. We can build a fire so the blade'll be hot."

"Only bawlin' I'm liable to do is when that wine runs out," Carl said, "if the cap'n don't drink it all first."

Will handed the bottle back to Carl, eyeing the bandage and the dried blood down Carl's sleeve. "Go fetch the knife," he said quietly, dreading the chore of digging for a bullet.

"You never did say what happened to the girl," Billy remarked, swinging away to find the knife.

Will turned south, toward Santa Elena Canyon. A setting sun bathed the basin with soft pink light. "I rode with her down to the river," he replied. "Sent her back to her people, where she belongs."

Carl grunted around a mouthful of plum wine. "She was a right pretty little thing when she was washed off." He gave Will a wink of conspiracy. " 'Course, you already knowed that, Cap'n. I see you lookin' at her from time to time."

"Let's get that slug out," Will said, perhaps a bit too quickly to sound casual. Changing the subject would help him forget about the tears Osate shed when they said goodbye at the river. If he could, he meant to forget about the girl entirely, though it promised to be a man-sized job after the tenderness they'd shared at the hidden spring.

He led his horse to one of the huts and began to strip his

saddle from the animal's back. The dun had carried him hundreds of hard miles since they rode away from San Antonio to begin the manhunt, and now it showed. Saddle sores darkened the gelding's yellow coat when he pulled his rig and tossed it in front of the adobe. Raw abrasions where the girth rubbed its skin seeped fluid. Will guessed the big horse had lost more than a hundred pounds of flesh, existing on scant grass and a few handfuls of grain that was quickly depleted. He rubbed behind one of the dun's ears. "Sorry I had to use you so rough, hoss," he whispered. "Wouldn't of done it if I'd had a choice."

Leon was gathering dry limbs for the fire when Will hobbled his horse in the cottonwoods. Will trudged slowly for the circle of stones Billy made for the fire, feeling too weary for the unpleasant task he would face when the knife blade was hot. Carl rested against the wall of a hut, nursing his bottle.

"You drink up enough courage?" he asked when he reached Carl.

Carl nodded, sadly contemplating the last of the wine. "Worst sight on earth is an empty jug, Cap'n. I ain't worried about that little bitty piece of lead comin' out. It's that long ride back to the closest saloon."

Will knelt beside Carl and untied the bandage, fingering open the tear in Carl's skin. "Don't look too awful deep," he said when he could see the hollow into the muscle. "Soon as Billy gets that knife hot, I'll get it outta there."

Carl chuckled softly and shook his head. "I've said this before, Cap'n. This has got to be the shittiest job in Texas, maybe even the whole world. Here we sit in the middle of nowhere, earnin' a lousy twenty dollars a month sleepin' on hard ground. No women or whiskey, and nothin' much to eat. Me an' Billy nearly got our asses shot off, and your face looks like you been in fight with a mountain lion. My boots are wore out, and now I've got a hole in my best shirt. Why the hell does any man want to be a Texas Ranger?"

Will rocked back on his boot heels and thought about Carl's question. "Hard to say, Carl. I 'spect most of us have got different reasons. In the beginning I took this job when I couldn't find any other kind of work. First year or two, I figured I'd lost my mind to want this kind of life. But after a spell, I reckon it sorta growed on me. I got to likin' it . . . bein' on the move from place to place without anything to tie me down. Lots of times I'd get to wishin' I had a good woman, and a place to call home. But mostly I like what I'm doin'. It makes some sense. This part of the country is chock full of hardcases and thieves who'll take any advantage they can. Somebody has to keep 'em in line. I know it sounds kinda funny, but I hardly ever think about the rotten pay, or the risks. I get this feelin' inside when I've done my job. I reckon you could call it pride.'' He cleared his throat after the speech was made. "It's kinda hard to explain. . . .''

Carl's cold green eyes were fixed on Will. For a while he simply stared. "I suppose I feel 'bout the same way,'' he said in a faraway voice, as if talking to himself. "I've always been the sort of gent who hated a bully or a card cheat. Makes me feel damn good when I put 'em in their place with this badge. Even the killin' feels good sometimes. Some of the sorry sons of bitches deserve to die. Hell, Cap'n, I suppose it's the truth that I like this shitty job. Don't know what else I'd do with myself. I damn sure ain't a farmer.''

Will watched the sky darken above the basin. "There's still a place for men like us, Carl,'' he said, "workin' for the Texas Rangers. As long as there's lawbreakers who use a gun to get what they want, this state needs us. It ain't very fancy work, but it's a job that has to be done.''

Carl grunted and tipped the bottle to his mouth, draining the last of the wine. Then he sighed and smacked his lips. "Let's get that goddamn hunk o' lead out,'' he said, glancing down to his shoulder. "Wouldn't want Major Peoples to think I wasn't worth twenty a month with just one good arm.''

At dawn Will led the column of riders north, across the western edge of the Chisos Mountains. Four Comancheros wearing gags and wrist irons were tied to the backs of their horses. Their pace was slow, for the Rangers' business was finished here. Will was headed back to Fort Davis to requisition fresh horses from the army, and to show Major Ranald Copeland some of the men his troops couldn't find. The ride back to the state capital would take weeks. Will promised his men frequent rest stops along the way, and plenty of good food and whiskey at the state's expense.

For the first few hours, he rode along listening to the creak of saddle leather and the hoofbeats of slow-moving horses, his mind at rest now that a difficult assignment was behind them. Later in the morning thoughts of the beautiful Indian girl would steal into his mind. When he tried to think of other things, he failed miserably. He wondered if he'd made a poor choice, sending her away. A time was nearing when age would take him from the seat of his saddle, when failing eyesight and slower reflexes rendered him of little use to a peacekeeping force. Perhaps old age might have been more enjoyable with Osate.

He turned back in the saddle once, gazing off toward the mountains of Mexico.

Chapter
Twenty-four

In his prime, Charlie had been tough as nails. Now age bent his back and thinned his hair on top, slackening his muscles. His face was still leathery from too much sun and wind, though his job kept him inside most of the time, hunched over a cluttered desk. But beneath the wrinkles and folds of loose skin, he was every bit as tough as he ever was. When he looked at Will the way he did now, the toughness was mirrored in his eyes.

"That's about it, Charlie," Will said, toying with a shot glass resting on his knee. They had been sitting beside the fireplace for several hours while Will gave his report to the major. Half a bottle of brandy had been emptied. The fire burned low. Outside the darkened windowpanes at Ranger headquarters, a cold north wind howled, rattling loose glass.

"I'd call it a job well done," Charlie offered, adding more brandy to their glasses. "A hell of a lot of bloodshed, but I suppose it couldn't be helped. The governor will be grinning from ear to ear when I tell him about it. He'll plan a public hanging for those gunrunners. The trial will be a mere formality. Stuffed ballot boxes are what he's really after. There's been a clamor to run him out of office. I hear the Democrats are working hard to defeat Davis. If Davis wins, Company C deserves some of the credit."

"I'm not much on politics," Will said, sipping brandy.

"Nobody wants the job, except for the crooks. A man has to be a thief at heart to run for office in times like these. I try to keep my nose out of it as much as I can. Congratulations for completing a rough assignment, Will. I knew I selected the right men for the problem down there.'' Charlie frowned thoughtfully. ''A couple of your men have kept me in hot water more than once. Graves has the worst record, I think. Tumlinson is almost as bad. However, I trust your judgment. If you say their performance has been within the boundaries of the law, I'll take your word for it.''

''Just barely,'' Will whispered, remembering. ''They're good men for the job you've given us. You don't know what it's like out there some of the time, when it's just them or us.''

The major stood up abruptly, eyes boring holes into Will. ''Like hell I don't! You think I'm some tinhorn? I've been to all those wild places, back when the Rangers first started. I fought the Kiowas and Comanch' with a damn muzzle-loader and cap-an'-ball pistols that misfired half the time. Don't tell me I don't know what it's like!''

Charlie's outburst caught Will off guard. ''Take it easy, Charlie,'' he protested. ''I was only sayin' I need men like Leon and Carl and Billy when we're in a tight spot.''

Some of the color drained from the major's face and the fire cooled behind his eyes. ''Sorry, Will. Honestly, I'm sick of this desk job and the goddamn paperwork. I get riled up when I shouldn't. I feel like I've been put out to pasture like an old horse. I know it isn't your fault when I blow up now and then. And I know you need hard men to police that border country. The Rio Grande is the last stretch of lawlessness in this state, most of it. Some of those towns below the river are nothing but a roosting place for killers from every other state in the union. If I had my way, we'd triple the size of the companies down there, but the legislature won't authorize any more men for the Rangers. We've simply got to do the job with the men we have. If it requires a few trigger-happy malcontents like Graves and Tumlinson, then so be it. So long as they don't break the law, I'll stew in the hot water when I have to. But remember, I'm looking to you to make damn sure your men operate within the laws of Texas.''

"There are times when it's by the skin of their teeth," Will recalled.

Charlie eased back down in his chair. "I suppose it's always been that way to some degree. Back in the fifties, outposts were far apart. Lots of places we were the only law there was. We might catch a horse thief or a man wanted for a killing in another town when our orders said we were needed someplace else, so we strung up the ones we had and went lookin' for the next bunch. There weren't many judges or jailhouses back then. We became the judge and jury. We couldn't simply turn them loose. A state judge might call that breakin' the law ourselves, if it happened now. But we did what we had to do under those circumstances. I'll never fault my men for doing the same. A man has to make some quick decisions when he wears a badge. There isn't always time to think about what a judge would have to say about the way a Ranger handles himself. It's hard to make a judge understand sometimes. You do the best you can, and I'll back you every step of the way."

"I know that, Charlie," Will said quietly. "You've always stood behind us. I'm not lookin' forward to the day when I'll be answering to somebody else."

The major looked up at the fireplace mantle, where his commission as a Texas Ranger was framed. "May not be much longer," he said in a faraway voice. "I've been thinking about retiring. I hate the paperwork."

"I've been thinkin' about hangin' it up myself, Charlie. I've been worryin' that I'm gettin' too old for this job. Gettin' slower, and my eyes ain't what they used to be. If I wait too long, it could get me an early grave. Trouble is, I don't know what else to do. Rangerin' is all I've known since the war."

Charlie scowled. "You're still a young man, Will. You've got plenty of time left. When age starts to slow a man down, he does more thinking before he makes a move. Use your brain instead of your gun. Let the younger men do the fighting."

"I reckon that's what I'm doing now—letting my men take most of the risks. It was a fool-headed stunt when I tangled with that big Comanche, and I know it now. He was stronger, and a hell of a lot quicker. I wasn't thinking when I went after him alone, an' it was damn near a fatal mistake.''

The major laughed softly. ''It'll be a good reminder. You'll remember what it was like to stare death in the eye. You're a tough hombre, and that's one reason why I gave you a captain's rank, but no matter how tough a man is, there's always somebody out there who's a little tougher. The trick is learning how to stay alive when the man you're after may be your equal. Outthink the bastards and you'll live to a ripe old age, so you can shuffle papers across a damn desk like me.''

''I learned a lesson from that renegade,'' Will replied. ''I found out an ordinary man doesn't stand a chance when things are equal between him an' a Comanche. I got to my weapon first. Otherwise, he'd have killed me. I'm alive because of the luck of the draw—my hand was closer to that rifle.''

Charlie seemed amused. ''I've always said I'd rather be lucky than good. But even a lucky man's luck plays out once in a while, so it's better to outsmart an adversary in the first place. Use your experience. Think faster than the other man and you won't have to count on luck.''

Will emptied his glass. ''I'd better be going. The bed at that hotel looked mighty inviting. Much obliged for the brandy, Charlie. And when you give your report to the governor, tell him the men we had to kill wouldn't allow it any other way.''

The major stood and offered a handshake. ''I'll explain it. I don't expect too much displeasure from him over the death toll. He can claim bringing an end to the Indian problem out west, and that oughta satisfy him. He knows it'll look good in the newspapers around the state.''

Will took his coat from a peg by the door, taking note of the bullet hole in one of the tails of the duster. ''That renegade slug was meant for me,'' he joked, showing the hole to Charlie while he sleeved into the tattered garment. ''Coulda been my skin.''

Charlie clumped over to the door to show Will out. ''That's

a nasty slice above your ear. Remember what I told you about using your head? Well, I didn't mean it quite that way."

"I was listening," Will replied, unable to crack a grin over the major's intended humor, remembering scenes from the hand-to-hand battle with Iron Horse. "I've got the renegade chief to thank for that knot on my skull. He almost did me in, Charlie. Never been that close to dyin' before that I recall. Strongest son of a bitch I ever had my hands on. I couldn't budge him. I got lucky when I reached for that rifle."

Charlie looked Will in the eye. "You've tangled with enough big men to know you can't outmuscle them. Like I said, you've got to outthink them. You'll live a lot longer if you follow my advice."

Will buttoned the front of his coat, hearing the wind whistle under a crack at the bottom of the door. The walk to the hotel up Congress Street would be facing the wind. "I still say there's a bit of luck involved," he argued, reaching for the latch when his collar was turned up and his hat was tilted off the scar above his right ear. He heard Charlie laugh.

"I knew a gambler one time," the major began. "Claimed he was the luckiest man on earth. Along with all that luck, he tried to cheat the odds. Tried to sleeve an ace up in Fort Worth. One of the players saw him and pulled a gun. Now right then, if that gambler had all the luck he claimed, the bullet wouldn't have killed him. I say you make your own luck, good and bad."

Will shrugged. "I gave up tryin' to figure it out a long time ago. Whatever it is that pulls me through, I was damn glad to have it in those mountains. Call it what you want." He opened the door and met a brisk blast of winter wind. "G'night, Charlie. We'll be headed back to San Antone in the morning." Leaning into an icy gust, he started down the boardwalk.

Lantern light from the windows of the Travis Saloon cast golden squares in front of him as he trudged for the hotel. Carl and Leon would still be there, catching up on their drinking. Billy would be ensconced in his hotel room with the prettiest saloon girl he could find. Carl and Leon would seek the same pleasant diversions, but not until Carl's powerful thirst for spirits had been quenched. Will chuckled to himself, wondering if there was enough whiskey in Austin to satisfy Carl. It seemed unlikely.

He paused in front of a saloon window when he saw Leon and Carl at a table, seated beside a couple of painted saloon waitresses. If he was any judge, the two Rangers were recounting their exploits in far west Texas. They both looked better in the lantern's glow after baths, hair trims, and shaves. Carl's shoulder was healing, though Will doubted the big Ranger paid any heed to the soreness tonight. With a bellyful of barley juice, he wouldn't notice it again until morning.

Will tented his shoulders and resumed his march into the wind with his hands shoved deeply in his coat pockets. He thought about the well-deserved celebration his men were enjoying. The success of the assignment below Fort Davis was certainly worthy of a night on the town. And while the men in his company were regarded as misfits compared to other lawmen across the state, Will knew they were a special breed who could match the violence they were asked to curtail along the Texas-Mexico border. Graveyards all over South Texas were full of peace officers who didn't have the stomach for it.

About the Author

Frederic Bean is the author of several Westerns, including *Bloody Sunday*, *Killing Season*, and *Hangman's Legacy* for Fawcett. He lives in Austin, Texas.